PUFFIN BOOKS

SAVING STARLIGHT

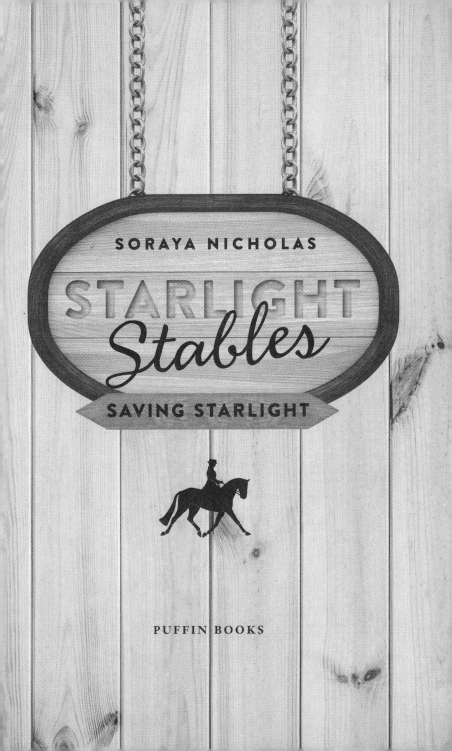

SORAYA NICHOLAS

STARLIGHT
Stables

SAVING STARLIGHT

PUFFIN BOOKS

PUFFIN BOOKS

UK | USA | Canada | Ireland | Australia
India | New Zealand | South Africa | China

Penguin Books is part of the Penguin Random House group of companies
whose addresses can be found at global.penguinrandomhouse.com.

Penguin
Random House
Australia

First published by Penguin Random House Australia Pty Ltd, 2016.

10 9 8 7 6 5 4 3 2 1

Text copyright © Soraya Nicholas, 2016.

The moral right of the author has been asserted.

All rights reserved. Without limiting the rights under copyright reserved above, no part of this
publication may be reproduced, stored in or introduced into a retrieval system, or transmitted, in
any form or by any means (electronic, mechanical, photocopying, recording or otherwise), without
the prior written permission of both the copyright owner and the above publisher of this book.

Design by Marina Messiha © Penguin Random House Australia Pty Ltd
Cover photograph © Caitlin Maloney, Ragamuffin Pet Photography
Author photograph p158 by Carys Monteath
Printed and bound in Australia by Griffin Press, an accredited ISO AS/NZS 14001 Environmental
Management Systems printer.

National Library of Australia Cataloguing-in-Publication data:

Nicholas, Soraya, author.
Starlight stables: saving starlight/Soraya Nicholas.

ISBN 978 0 1433 0866 9 (paperback)

For children.
Ponies – Juvenile fiction.
Horse shows – Juvenile fiction.
Friendship – Juvenile fiction.

A823.4

penguin.com.au

For Isabella, India & Emily, our beautiful, horse-crazy cover models! And for my goddaughter Amelia and friend Arabella, for being such great inspiration for my characters.

CHAPTER ONE

Jupiter

'She's amazing,' Katie said, her voice barely a whisper.

Poppy glanced across at her friend, smiling when she realised how in awe Katie was. She still found her Aunt Sophie incredible to watch and she'd been watching her for years, so she got why Katie and Milly couldn't take their eyes off her. Aunt Sophie was riding her beautiful big Warmblood gelding, Jupiter, in the arena at Starlight Stables, practising one of her dressage tests. The chestnut horse seemed to glide around the arena, his thickly muscled neck perfectly arched, strong legs carrying him gracefully, his change from walk to canter and

1

then back down to a forward-moving trot absolutely faultless.

'Do you think she'll win?' Milly asked. 'She has to, right? I mean, she's *crazy* good.'

Poppy bit down on her lip, gently chewing it. Aunt Sophie was good – Poppy personally thought she was the best – but then so was every other rider she'd be up against. 'I hope so,' she replied.

'I was reading in *HorseWyse* the other day that she's the one to beat at the Nationals,' Katie told them, still completely mesmerised. 'The article said that Jupiter is one of the oldest horses competing now, and that he has the most experience.'

Poppy was so excited about The National Dressage Championships. They were being held in Melbourne, which meant they were going to be right there watching her aunt, and Sophie has asked Poppy to be her groom! Although Katie and Milly would be in the crowd watching, Poppy was the only one actually helping to prepare Jupiter. She'd been reading everything she could about being a groom – it was going to be awesome.

It was less than four weeks until Sophie's big weekend, and Poppy's stomach was already flip-flopping like crazy about being involved. Most of the riders would have full-time grooms, but her aunt and uncle did everything without help, to keep costs down and to fund their young riders. This year the championships was in Melbourne, which was the only reason Poppy was able to go – her mum didn't have to pay for flights. She was going to stay over at Starlight Stables the night before the event to help out, and then travel with Sophie in the horse truck for the hour's drive into Melbourne.

'Do you think we'll ever be that good?' Katie asked, jolting her out of her daydreams.

Milly made a snorting noise that made Poppy giggle. 'You sound like a piglet!' she laughed.

'I've got more chance of turning into a piglet than ever being that good!' Milly said.

Katie rolled her eyes at Poppy. Milly was always such a drama queen.

'Are you excited about our show-jumping comp next weekend?' Poppy asked.

'Ohmygod, so excited!' Milly jumped up, then quickly sat down when Poppy tugged on her arm.

'Stay still,' Poppy hissed, keeping hold of Milly's arm. 'Aunt Sophie said we could watch if we stayed quiet and didn't distract her.'

Milly made a face – a half smile, half grimace. 'Sorry.'

Milly could never sit still; she was always leaping around and coming up with crazy ideas. Poppy glanced at Katie, thinking how different her two friends were. Katie's hair was as blonde as Milly's was dark, as straight as Milly's was curly. They were both completely horse crazy, but Katie was quieter and more serious.

Poppy loved them both, and she still couldn't believe they'd been friends for less than a year. Aunt Sophie and Uncle Mark had given Poppy her own pony, Crystal, when she'd come for the Christmas holidays. At the same time they'd told her they were giving two other deserving riders scholarships, and that was when she'd met Katie and Milly. They'd spent almost all of January together.

There were only two months to go until the Christmas holidays started again, and Poppy couldn't wait to have another long stay at Starlight Stables. She was lucky to visit every second weekend, and they had all just had a week of the last school holidays at the farm, but over summer Poppy had an entire month or more to spend every single day with Crystal and her friends, and she couldn't wait!

'Sophie!' Poppy looked behind her when she heard Uncle Mark calling out. His frown told her something was wrong. She hardly ever saw him without a big smile on his face, so she knew something was up straightaway.

Poppy exchanged glances with the other two and then turned to watch Sophie. She was still focused on her dressage, oblivious to Mark.

'Sophie!' His yell was louder this time and he strode to the edge of the arena, obviously agitated.

Aunt Sophie looked annoyed as she halted Jupiter and walked him over to Mark. Poppy watched them discuss something and saw an expression of shock on Sophie's face as Uncle Mark gestured back at the house. Her aunt quickly dismounted. She was pulling her gloves off, which was a sure sign that she was finished riding. But what would be so important that she'd stop riding before finishing the test she was practising? And why did Mark look so cross?

'Poppy!' Her aunt waved her over urgently.

Poppy jumped up. They were sitting on a

wooden bench seat on the far side of the arena, and she had to run to the entrance where Sophie was waiting.

'What's wrong?' Poppy asked the second she got there, breathing hard.

Mark had already headed back to the house, the fast walk–run thing he was doing at odds with how relaxed he usually was. Poppy's heart was thumping loud, waiting to hear the bad news.

'Poppy, I . . .'

'It's not my mum, is it?' she blurted out, wrapping her arms around herself. 'Has something happened?'

'No, sweetheart, nothing like that,' Sophie said, passing her the reins and giving her a kind smile. 'Something important has come up. We have a visitor that I need to meet with. Nothing for you to worry about.'

'Oh, sure. Okay,' Poppy muttered, feeling silly for jumping to conclusions.

'Can you take Jupiter for me? Keep him walking for maybe ten minutes, then take him back to his stable and brush him down for me.'

Poppy could hardly believe what she was hearing.

Her take Jupiter? 'Do you just want me to lead him?'

'No, silly.' Aunty Sophie smiled. 'I want you to hop on and cool him down for me. Let him stretch out after all that collected work in the arena.' She frowned at the look on Poppy's face. 'I thought you'd be excited about riding him?'

'Excited?' Poppy stammered. 'I could do cartwheels I'm so excited!' She giggled and held the reins tight. 'I just didn't think you'd want me on his back.'

Sophie put a hand on her shoulder and squeezed. 'Poppy, you're a fantastic little rider. Enjoy it.'

Her aunt turned and hurried after Mark, leaving Poppy standing with her jaw just about hitting the ground. She was about to ride Jupiter! Poppy ran a hand down his neck, admiring the massive 17.2-hand high gelding.

'What was all that about?' Milly asked, running up behind her with Katie hot on her heels.

'Nothing really, they just have a visitor or something,' Poppy said, still in awe of the horse she was holding.

'Do you have to take him back?' Katie asked.

A grin spread slowly over Poppy's face. 'Nope.

She wants me to ride him.'

Milly shook her head. 'No way!'

'Yes way. Now, who's giving me a leg up? There's no way I can mount him from the ground.'

Milly elbowed Katie out of the way and quickly bent down to take her leg. 'Hope I can get you high enough.'

Poppy threw the reins over Jupiter's head. 'Ready.' She put her left leg in Milly's hands.

'One, two, *three*!'

'Milly!' cried Poppy as she swooshed through the air and landed with a thud on Jupiter's back. Her bottom hit the saddle way harder than she'd wanted it to, but Milly had boosted her so high! Thankfully, Jupiter didn't even flinch.

'Sorry,' Milly said with a giggle. 'You look so little up there. He probably doesn't even realise there's anybody in the saddle!'

Poppy poked out her tongue before settling into the amazingly comfy dressage saddle. The seat was a lot deeper than her general-purpose saddle, and it made her sit differently. She put the stirrups up as they were way too long for her, and gathered the reins up only a little – she was supposed to be cooling him down, which meant letting him stretch his neck out.

'What's it like up there?' Katie asked.

Poppy grinned and looked down. 'A long way to fall!' She laughed, amazed at how relaxed Jupiter was. Some competition horses were so highly strung, but he had always been so lovely. When he was at a competition he was in full show-off mode, but at home he was very chilled out.

Poppy nudged him in the sides gently. She had to remember that he was a highly trained horse and was used to very subtle leg signals from her aunt. He obliged and walked forward straightaway, but it felt so different.

'His stride is huge!' she said to Milly and Katie who were walking alongside her. 'It feels awesome.'

Poppy sat as straight as she could, nudging him every few steps with the inside of her legs. She felt a million dollars sitting astride Sophie's horse, and she still couldn't believe she'd been trusted enough to ride him. There was a chance Sophie could qualify for the Olympic dressage team on Jupiter, which meant he was probably one of the most valuable dressage horses in Melbourne, or even Australia!

She took a deep breath, calmed herself down. She always got crazy-excited thinking about her aunt making the Olympic team one day, because no matter how much Aunt Sophie tried to stay quiet about some things, Poppy knew it was her aunt's dream and had heard her talking about it with Uncle Mark.

'You should trot,' Milly suggested. 'See what it's like.'

'Uh-uh,' Poppy said firmly, not about to let Milly convince her of some crazy idea. 'She told me to walk him for ten minutes, and that's exactly what I'm going to do.'

Milly groaned. 'You're so boring.'

'That's why Mrs D asked *Poppy* to ride Jupiter and not you!' Katie said.

While her friends laughed and joked around, Poppy concentrated on Jupiter, feeling his stride, the way he stepped out and covered so much of the ground. Riding him was elegant, felt so different to her fun, zippy little pony. If she just shut her eyes . . .

'Milly!' she squealed, pulling Jupiter to a sudden halt. 'I almost ran you over!'

'Um, that's what you get for riding with your eyes closed, stupid.'

Poppy ignored her and nudged Jupiter back into a walk. She kept going for a while, happy that he was stretching out his neck and seemed as relaxed as he usually was for Sophie after a work-out. When she was certain they'd been going for at least ten minutes, Poppy rode him towards the arena exit, knowing her friends would follow. She could have dismounted and lead him, but she wanted to spend as much time on Jupiter as she could, and that meant riding him all the way back to the stables.

'Wait up!' Katie called.

Poppy didn't slow down – she was loving the feel of his long strides, and it was only a couple of minutes back to the barn anyway. When it was time to dismount she did it slowly, landing with a big thump on the ground from so high up.

'Good boy,' she praised, patting his neck and slipping the reins over his ears when he dipped his chestnut head for a cuddle. Poppy stroked his cheek and dropped a kiss to his nose just as the others joined her.

'I'm so jealous,' Milly said.

'I know,' Poppy replied smugly. It wasn't often that Milly didn't figure out a way to get what she wanted, and she knew how much it would be annoying her.

She tied Jupiter outside his stall and removed his bridle then saddle. Milly appeared at her side with a brush and started on his body, and Poppy carefully picked out his hooves, making sure they were clean. Aunt Sophie was very particular about his care, making sure he was treated like a star. She was always telling Poppy that he was a top athlete, and that meant taking extra care of his grooming, feeding and exercise. He even had massages every week.

'Want me to grab his rug?' Katie called out.

'Yep, thanks,' Poppy replied, dropping the hoof pick and grabbing a soft brush to do his face. 'I think he loves all this fuss.'

'Yeah, I reckon,' Milly said, still working on his gleaming coat. He'd been sweating but his summer coat was so fine that a brush was all he needed. If Aunt Sophie had done her full work-out on him, they'd have had to hose him down.

Katie flung his rug on, and Poppy did the front

up while Katie did the back. It was just a light cover to keep the sun and bugs off him, and once Jupiter was ready Poppy untied him and led him outside, letting him into the paddock alongside the barn. It wasn't so big that he could gallop around and hurt himself, but it meant he could stretch his legs a little and pick at some grass.

'Do you recognise that car?' Katie asked suddenly.

Poppy slung Jupiter's lead rope over her shoulder and squinted at the white vehicle over in the Delaney's driveway. It was parked close to the house, which made it hard for her to read the small black writing on the side, but it had her curious. 'Can you take this back to the tack room?' Poppy asked, holding the rope out to Katie. 'I'm going to take a closer look.'

Milly's eyebrows popped up. 'Can I come?'

'If you want,' Poppy replied, still staring at the car and knowing in her heart that something just wasn't right. Nothing usually upset Mark, he was always so chilled out, which made Poppy all the more worried.

'I'll take this back then catch you up,' Katie said.

Poppy brushed her dirty hands on her jodhpurs as she and Milly walked across the grass, past the towering blue gums between the barn and the farmhouse. As they got closer she read the writing: *ANZ Bank*. She glanced at Milly.

'Why would someone from a bank be here?' Milly asked, frowning.

Poppy shook her head. 'I don't know, but I'm going to find out.'

Something was up, something big, and she needed to know what was going on.

'Oooh, how? What are we going to do?'

Poppy stopped and stared at her friend. She didn't exactly have a plan, but . . .

'I'm going to eavesdrop. You guys stay here just in case Aunt Sophie's not in there and comes looking for us. I don't want her to know that we're trying to figure out what's going on.'

Milly looked impressed, responding with a wide smile. 'That sounds like the perfect plan.'

Poppy wasn't so sure. It sounded more like a Milly plan. She dug her nails into her palms. 'I'll be back soon.'

CHAPTER TWO

Caught Out

Poppy silently took her boots off and let herself in through the back door, tiptoeing across the carpet and pausing at the end of the hallway. She could hear voices coming from the kitchen. She pressed her back to the wall and listened, breathing as quietly as she could. The last thing she wanted was for her aunt or uncle to hear her.

'I don't think you appreciate how much trouble you're in here.'

The words were muffled, but she'd heard them. Or at least she was certain that's what she'd heard. It was a man's voice, deeper than her Uncle Mark's, and she didn't recognise it. Poppy had no idea what he meant, but it didn't sound good.

She padded silently towards the kitchen. The door was shut, which was weird – they never usually closed doors in the house – and she took a big gulp of air before pressing her ear to it. Poppy's heart was thudding, the noise loud in her own ears. She hoped that it wasn't actually that loud outside her body otherwise they'd know she was here for sure!

'We can extend you one month, but if we don't start seeing –'

'I appreciate the offer, and we'll make sure there are no missed payments,' Uncle Mark interrupted in a loud, confident voice. 'This is just a minor hiccup.'

'I'd hardly call losing a big sponsor a minor hiccup,' the man said. 'Especially when you can't give me the name of another company that might step in to assist you.'

No sponsor? Poppy could hardly breathe, even her bones seemed to ache. How could Aunt Sophie have lost her sponsor? She was sponsored by one of the biggest horse-feed companies in Australia. Their name was splashed over everything Sophie owned – her horse truck, her show rugs, her riding clothes. Why would they drop her when she was doing so well, when she was so close to doing better than she'd ever done before? They'd backed her right from the start of her career!

'Eeek!' Poppy squeaked, jumping when something pushed her leg from behind. She spun around to find her aunt and uncle's big dog standing behind her, his shaggy tail wagging. He'd butted her with his nose and he was about to do it again.

Just as she whispered sternly 'No!' to him, the door was flung open. Poppy stumbled forward and sprawled on the kitchen floor. Casper stood over her, his tongue lolling out as he gave her a big doggy smile.

'Poppy?' Uncle Mark was frowning down at her.
Ooops.

'I was just, um . . .' Poppy stammered, not sure what to say.

'Here, up you hop,' Aunt Sophie said, stepping forward and extending a hand.

Poppy's face felt on fire. She held out her hand and grasped Sophie's, hauling herself up as gracefully as she could and glancing at the two strange men seated at the table. As she looked at them they both stood, collecting their paperwork with faces that made her want to look away. There was nothing kind in their expressions, and it made goosebumps break out across her body.

'We'll expect to hear from you within thirty days,' the tallest of the men said.

Poppy slunk over to the bench and reached for a glass, pouring some water. She didn't know what to do and it seemed best to pretend like she'd actually been coming in to the kitchen for a reason.

Uncle Mark led them out and she let out a big breath and waited for Aunt Sophie to come back into the room. But her aunt just stood still in the doorway, her back to Poppy.

'Is, um, everything okay?' Poppy asked, cringing as she said the words and wishing she'd just kept her mouth shut. *Duh, everything was so obviously not okay!*

Aunt Sophie turned, and to Poppy's horror there were tears in her eyes. She'd never, ever seen her aunt cry, except at her dad's funeral, and Poppy didn't know what to do. She put her glass down and took a few awkward steps forward.

'Everything will be fine,' Sophie said, as she brushed her knuckles past her eyes and flashed

Poppy a smile. 'We're just having a little bit of financial trouble, that's all.'

Uncle Mark stepped back into the room then. 'Poppy, put the kettle on would you? I need a strong cup of coffee.'

He slumped down at the table, and Poppy quickly did as he'd asked, pulling out a couple of mugs and spooning some coffee in. It was nice to have something to do because she'd never seen her aunt and uncle so sad and she had no idea what she was supposed to say. If only she'd just stayed outside instead of coming in to investigate!

Her aunt was standing with her hands planted on the back of a chair, and Mark sat silently opposite her.

'Thanks,' he said when Poppy set their coffees down in front of them.

She watched as they exchanged glances, wondering if she could just run back out to the horses and forget she'd heard anything at all.

'Poppy, sweetheart, I think you should sit down,' Uncle Mark said.

She slid into a chair. 'Is there anything I can do?'

Mark sighed. 'Sophie lost her sponsor about a

month ago. We've been trying to secure a new deal, form a new partnership with another company, but for now we're having to fund everything ourselves, which means taking out a new loan. The bank is seriously breathing down our necks.'

Poppy folded her hands together tightly under the table. She looked from Mark to Sophie and back again. They were treating her like an adult, talking to her like this, and she didn't want to say the wrong thing or do something stupid like burst into tears.

'What does that mean for Starlight Stables?' she asked.

Aunt Sophie reached out and placed a hand on her shoulder, her touch warm. Her aunt and uncle had been so kind and good to her and she hated to see them so worried.

'Poppy, we have a lot of debt. There's the mortgage on this place, the loan we took out for Mark to buy the local vet practice, and we had to buy the sponsor's half share in Prince, otherwise he was going to be offered up for sale.'

Thank goodness they'd been able to keep Prince! Her aunt's new young horse was already showing signs of being a star in the making.

'It's hurt us big time,' her aunt said, 'and that's without the loan on the three new ponies.'

Poppy's blood ran cold. She meant *their* ponies. *Crystal. Joe. Cody.*

'I don't understand,' she managed to say. 'Why would they stop sponsoring you?'

'Because the sponsor company is in trouble. They had to cancel all their sponsorship deals to stop their business going under. It's just one of those things.'

One of those things! Poppy's heart was racing again. 'What are you going to do?'

Mark grimaced. 'Worst-case scenario is that we have to sell the farm,' he said, holding up his hand when Poppy gasped. 'But we won't let it come to that. We're going to find a new sponsor, and everything will be fine. I won't be selling this place without a fight!'

Poppy's breath was shallow, her lungs hardly working. 'You can't lose the farm. I can't lose Crystal,' she whispered.

Sophie walked up behind her and put her arms around her neck, her cheek to Poppy's hair. 'I will do everything I can to make sure you never lose

Crystal, sweetheart. This isn't something you need to be worrying about.'

But she was. There was no way she could hear news like this and not be upset, not be worried. 'Should we still all go to the show-jumping competition next weekend?' she asked. 'Because if it's too much . . . ' her voice trailed off.

Sophie dropped a kiss on the top of Poppy's head. 'Of course. Just like I'm going to ride better than I've ever ridden before at the National Champs. Nothing is going to stop us, at least not without a darn good fight.'

Poppy stood up, needing to get out of the kitchen. She felt like there wasn't enough air inside for her to breathe. 'Can I go now?'

Uncle Mark nodded when she looked at him. 'Go ride, enjoy your pony. This is for us to worry about, not you. Just go be a kid.'

Poppy bristled, hating hearing that.

How could she not worry about this?! Without Crystal . . . tears sprang into her eyes at the thought of being without her beloved horse. She felt guilty, because her aunt and uncle were talking about losing their farm, but the thought of losing her own pony . . . She bit hard on her bottom lip.

With one last look at Sophie and Mark, she walked from the room, running when she reached the hall. Poppy yanked on her boots and ran as fast she could, arms pumping, lungs screaming, as she pushed herself faster and faster. Casper was by her side, his big body stretched out as he raced her. When she finally couldn't run any longer, Poppy flopped to the ground, curling into a ball on the grass. The tears started in a steady trail down her cheeks until her entire body was shaking and heaving with sobs that she couldn't control. And then Casper was with her, licking her face, thumping her with his paw and whining. He finally curled up beside her and she buried her face into his thick fur, crying like she'd never cried in her life before.

'Poppy?'

Poppy groaned and slowly opened her eyes. The second she did it she wished she'd just kept them shut, the bright light hurt so much. She bet her eyes were red and puffy.

'Ow,' she muttered when her comfy fur pillow

stood up and her head hit the ground.

'Pops?'

She looked up and saw Milly and Katie standing over her. Milly was holding out a hand and when she didn't grasp it, both her friends dropped to the grass beside her. Poppy hadn't realised how far she'd run, but looking around now she could see she was quite a long way from the house.

'Are you okay?' Katie asked, her voice soft as she reached out and put an arm around her. 'What happened?'

'We were waiting for you and when you never came and Mrs D said you'd left the house an hour ago, we decided to come looking,' Milly said.

Poppy couldn't believe she'd fallen asleep curled up with Casper, but all the sleep in the world wasn't going to help her deal with what her aunt and uncle had told her.

'Sophie lost her sponsor and now they could lose the farm,' she blurted, surprised she had any tears left when fresh ones flooded her eyes. Poppy quickly explained what she'd found out, knowing how upset they'd both be.

'What can we do?' Katie asked. 'There must be

something. We can't just sit around waiting, hoping that our ponies don't get sold.'

Poppy loved that Katie was so practical in emergency situations. Just like when they'd been planning to look for the stolen horses, riding over to Old Smithy's place, she was so calm when things were bad.

'I said the same thing, but I don't know what we can do. I mean, I have a bit of pocket money, but nothing much,' Poppy said. They had an old lady in the house beside them at home, and she paid Poppy fifteen dollars a week to walk her dog on school days, but . . . she did a quick calculation. *Actually* . . .

'You know, I haven't touched my money since Christmas, and I've been saving a lot. I could have, like, three hundred dollars by now. Maybe more!' Trouble was, she had no idea how much Mark and Sophie would have paid for Crystal.

'Oooh, me too!' Milly said excitedly. 'I've been helping mum with her work, and she pays me a little bit, plus my grandparents gave me fifty dollars for my birthday. I've probably got about the same because I've been saving for a new pair of riding boots.'

Katie took her arm from around Poppy and sat back. 'Guys, I don't want to say this, but, um, I don't think that amount of money will help.'

'Why?' Milly asked.

Poppy had a feeling she knew what Katie was going to say.

'I read *HorseWyse* all the time, including all the For Sale adverts. I know that good ponies cost thousands, and that's what they would have paid for ours. A few hundred dollars each probably isn't going to make a difference.'

'No, you're wrong,' Milly was defiant, glaring at Katie like she was the enemy.

'She's only telling the truth,' Poppy said before Milly could get too cross with Katie.

'Well, the truth sucks.' Milly slammed her fist against the ground and stood up. 'Any money we come up with has to help. I say we find out exactly how much we have, and we give it all to Mrs D.'

Poppy wasn't going to argue. Whatever they could do to help must be worth it. They just had to find out how much money they needed to make a difference, and fast.

'What if the farm is sold, though? Then where

could we keep them even if we *had* paid for them?' Katie asked, her eyes swimming with tears. 'My parents would never let me keep Cody, I know it.'

Poppy knew exactly what her mum would say, too. It would be a big fat *no*. Even if Poppy had it all worked out, found somewhere to keep Crystal and saved up her own money, it would still be *no*.

'Plus how would we pay for feed and covers and . . .'

'Shut up!' Milly yelled. 'Just shut up and stop making it sound like we're about to lose our ponies.'

'I forgot to tell you one other thing,' Poppy suddenly said. 'Prince. They've had to buy him from the sponsor, but I bet he'll be the first horse sold if they need to get more money together.'

A shiver ran up Poppy's spine. Aunt Sophie's new young horse was incredible, one of the most gorgeous horses Poppy had ever seen, and it would be awful if he was sold. Although not as awful as seeing Jupiter go to a new home. Poppy shuddered. She couldn't even stand thinking about it all.

'We're not going to let this happen,' Milly declared.

Poppy stared at her plucky friend, tried to inhale

some of her positive energy. 'Milly's right. There has to be something we can do.'

Katie sighed. 'I didn't mean to be negative. I just don't see how we can make a difference.'

'We can,' Milly told them, holding out her hand and looking first at Poppy then at Katie. 'Let's make a vow to do anything we can to save Starlight Stables, and our ponies.'

'I'm in,' Poppy said straightaway, placing her hand over Milly's.

'Me too,' Katie added, her warm palm covering Poppy's hand.

'Now let's go ride and forget all about this doom and gloom stuff for a while. I vote we go for a big gallop.'

Poppy grinned at Milly. Trust her to make them all feel better. 'Me too. Why don't we ask if we can go to the beach tomorrow? Then we can have a proper gallop along the wet sand.'

They all stood up and walked over to the stables with Casper trotting along ahead of them, leading the way. Poppy looked around, breathed in the fresh country air and smiled at the big blue gum trees filled with birdlife, the endless paddocks stretching out around them, grass still green from the beautiful warm spring they'd had. She had the best memories here at Starlight, and the thought of not coming here any more made her so sad. But they could do something, she just knew they could. Starlight Stables meant everything to her, and she knew her friends felt the same.

CHAPTER THREE

Brainstorming Time

Poppy was so tired her eyes felt like they were going to fall out of her head. She groaned as the truck lurched. She should be super excited about riding the horses at the beach, but she'd found it impossible to get to sleep the night before, worrying about the farm. When she'd finally drifted off she'd had a nightmare about Crystal being sold to Jessica, the mean girl they'd met at Starlight when they were preparing for their first big gymkhana. She hadn't been able to sleep after that.

'Come on, sleepyhead.' Aunt Sophie's voice made her eyes pop open.

If her aunt could sound happy and positive,

then so could she. Poppy rubbed her eyes with her knuckles and sat up straighter. She was sitting beside Sophie, while Katie and Milly were seated in the living area of the truck, where the other seats were.

A stamp of hooves made Poppy's heart beat faster, the sudden anticipation of her next ride helping her to push the worries away. If she didn't have much longer with Crystal, then she was going to make sure she enjoyed every single ride.

'Come on, let's get these horses unloaded and geared up,' Aunt Sophie said cheerily.

Poppy got down and opened the side door for the others. They waited for Sophie to lower the tailgate, then Milly was up first, taking Joe down. Katie was up next, unloading a perfectly behaved Cody, and then Crystal, followed by Jupiter.

'I'm going to take Jupiter for a nice long walk to stretch out, but you girls can do whatever you like. Race, canter, gallop, swim.' Sophie shrugged. 'Just have fun.'

Poppy ran the soft body brush over Crystal's grey coat once she was tied to the side of the truck, feeling every curve and indent of her horse. She picked out Crystal's hooves then saddled her up, taking her time to do the girth up loosely to start with before tightening it up completely and putting Crystal's bridle on. Then Poppy pulled on her gloves, clicked on her helmet and turned to wait for the others. Milly and Katie were both ready seconds later, and they mounted just as Sophie was checking her girth.

'What's with you girls today? You've hardly said boo,' Aunt Sophie said, leading Jupiter over to the side of the truck, climbing up and then mounting.

Poppy looked at Katie and Milly. She gulped. 'Um, it's just . . .'

'Poppy told us what happened!' Milly blurted. 'I'm sorry, Pops, but I can't keep it secret.'

Poppy groaned. Trust Milly. She gave her an evil stare, hoping she'd realise how much trouble she was in. The last thing Sophie needed was anything more to worry about.

'Oh sweetheart, if I'd wanted to keep it a secret, I'd have asked you not to say anything. It's okay that you told the girls,' Sophie said, giving Poppy a smile. 'Come on, let's head out and you can ask me any questions you want to.'

Aunt Sophie was always so kind and nice to them, except when she was drilling them in the arena and demanding perfection, and it made Poppy sad all over again. She still couldn't believe what was happening. Or what might happen.

'We want you to know that we're going to do anything, *anything*, to help out,' Milly blurted. Poppy just wanted to tell her to shut up but she bit her tongue to keep quiet.

'I'm really sorry, Mrs D,' Katie said in a quiet voice that didn't even sound like her.

'I still should have asked you before telling them,' Poppy said, riding close to Aunt Sophie up front as they headed down towards the beach. The trail was narrower as they approached, going up over the sand dune, and Crystal started to jig-jog with excitement.

'It's okay. We all need someone to talk to, and you confided in Milly and Katie. It's fine.'

Poppy wasn't so sure it was fine, but she decided to take her aunt's word for it.

'What I don't want is you girls worrying. Mark and I are taking care of things, and we wouldn't have even told you if Poppy hadn't overheard what

33

was happening yesterday,' Aunt Sophie continued. 'Where there's a will, there's a way, which I know is a silly old-fashioned saying, but it's true. I was a girl desperate for her own pony as a ten year old, with a dream to be a top rider when I grew up. The chances of that actually happening were slim to none, but I know firsthand that anything is possible.'

'Did you always know that you wanted to be a dressage rider?' Katie asked.

They were on the beach now and Crystal was snorting, still jig-jogging beneath Poppy, but she stayed firm with her, sitting deep in the saddle and not letting her start trotting.

'I knew that I wanted to spend my life in the saddle, and when I was a teenager I started riding dressage and loved it,' Aunt Sophie replied. 'My point is, it's okay to dream big. Don't ever let anyone tell you that what you're dreaming is stupid or unattainable, and don't ever think that you can't make it happen if you work hard and believe in yourself.'

'So it's not stupid to actually think we could get to the Olympics one day?' Milly asked, her usually hyper voice sounding a whole lot more serious.

'Not if you're prepared to work hard every day and train,' Aunt Sophie said. 'It's tough to get the top, Milly, but not impossible. And if you want to know a little secret, it's my dream, too. Every competition takes me a step closer to my goal of one day making the Olympic squad for dressage.'

'I just know you'll get a great new sponsor, Mrs D,' Katie piped up. 'And you'll *so* make the Olympics one day.'

Poppy nodded in agreement.

'I hope you're right, girls, about the sponsor part at least,' Aunt Sophie said. 'Now, who's up for a trot? I think I'll trot for a bit with you all, then when you're ready you can take off and have fun on your own.'

Poppy didn't need to ask Crystal twice. Her excitable pony bounced straight into a trot, fighting to go faster. Jupiter's trot was huge and covered so much ground, and Crystal was desperate to keep up with him.

'Sorry Mrs D!' Milly yelled as Joe went flying straight past them all in the fight for first place. His nose was thrust high, almost more determined than Milly was.

'Don't let him get away on you, Milly,' Aunt Sophie called back. 'It's okay to be in front of me, but only if you're the one asking for it. Don't let Joe forget who the boss is.'

It was something her aunt had told her when she first started riding. It was fine to enjoy your horse, to have a partnership and treat them kindly, but the rider still had to be the boss. Otherwise there was no control, and it was dangerous for the horse to think they were the one in charge of making decisions.

Milly reined Joe back in front of them, riding him in a circle, then joined the group again at a trot. They continued on for a few minutes, the ponies bouncing along beside Jupiter.

'Can we go now?' Poppy called out.

'Go for it, girls!'

Poppy pressed her legs to Crystal's side and rose out of the saddle in a cross-country gallop position. She had her stirrups at jumping length and she kept her heels pressed firmly down, hands steady as she let Crystal stretch out.

Katie and Milly cantered beside her across the damp sand, which was the safest part of the beach to ride their horses on.

'Go, Crystal!' Poppy whispered, urging her even faster until they were in a full gallop, her pony going as quickly as she could. Poppy was sure the horses loved it as much as they did, the freedom of galloping down the endless stretch of beach a true rush of adrenalin. The wind whipped hard against Poppy's face, the roar of the ocean was loud in her ears.

She was looking between Crystal's pricked ears, but she did glance sideways to check where the others were. Milly was hot on her heels, so she wrapped her legs even tighter against Crystal's side, not wanting to let her friend beat her. It hadn't started as a race, but it sure was now! Crystal was grunting because she was going so fast, loving the competition, and Poppy grinned when she heard Milly yell something at her. No one liked winning more than Milly, which made racing against her and winning all the better.

Out of nowhere Katie shot past them, in the lead by a nose. They were all galloping fast now, three abreast, racing over the sand.

'Katie!' Poppy cried, laughing as she loosened the reins even more to let Crystal go as fast as she could. She couldn't believe Cody was faster than both Crystal and Joe, but he was winning fair and square.

Milly was yelling something out, right on Crystal's heels, but the wind was so loud at the speed they were going that Poppy couldn't figure out what she was saying. They kept going, all three of them neck and neck. It was the most amazing feeling in the world.

'My legs are killing me,' Milly moaned, stretching out in the shade of an ancient-looking jacaranda tree beside Poppy. The tree had a gnarled trunk, and the purple flowers were so bright and beautiful against the blue sky as Poppy stared up.

'Imagine how Joe is feeling. He was the one doing all the hard work,' Poppy replied. She had to admit that her own legs were sore from standing out of the saddle for so long as they raced and raced.

'Tuck into your lunch, girls,' Aunt Sophie said, emerging from the other side of the truck with her hands full. She set two bags of food down beside them.

Poppy stomach rumbled just at the thought of

eating. She didn't care what it was, she'd just about eat a horse right now!

'Bacon and egg pie, tomato sandwiches and chocolate brownies,' Aunt Sophie announced, setting everything down. 'I couldn't sleep last night, so I got up and made myself useful instead!'

'Yum,' Poppy said, pushing Milly aside as they both jostled to get closer to her aunt. She unpacked the bag in front of them and soon Poppy was practically drooling.

'It was a great idea coming here today, girls. Just what I needed,' Sophie said, pulling out paper plates and passing them around. 'Training can get so serious and dull leading up to a competition, so it's good to have a change of scenery.'

Poppy reached over and grabbed a sandwich, wolfing it down while Aunt Sophie cut the pie.

'Best lunch ever, Mrs D,' Milly said through a mouthful of sandwich.

There was hardly a scrap of food left once they were finished. Poppy was absolutely stuffed when she put her plate down and leant back against the tree.

'Poor Mark, I told him there'd be leftovers!'

Sophie said with a laugh. 'You girls ate like hungry bears.'

They sat a while longer in the shade, the early summer weather perfect. It was warm but not too hot, and Poppy felt her eyes closing as she listened to the others talking.

'Oh, I forgot to tell you girls more about next Saturday,' Aunt Sophie said. 'They're offering a round-the-ring jumping class, plus a single jump contest with a cash prize for the winner.'

Poppy sat bolt upright. She'd hardly been listening, but that made her ears prick up like a pony's. 'What kind of cash prize?' she asked.

'The single jump class is big, about $500 I think, plus horse feed for a year. It'll be tough competition, with any rider under seventeen years old allowed to enter, but I'd love you all to give it a go.'

Poppy's mind was racing, thinking of how much she could help her aunt and uncle out if she won. It was a lot of money, more than she could earn in a year walking the neighbour's dogs!

'I'm going to win it.'

'I know I told you to dream big Poppy, but . . .'

Poppy clamped her hand over her mouth, her

face burning. 'Oops. I didn't realise I'd said it out loud.'

'I don't want to discourage you, Pops, because you're definitely good enough to win, but you girls are only twelve, and that means you're going to be up against riders who are years older than you.' Aunt Sophie started to clean up the lunch. 'If you want to win though, don't let me stop you. We'll saddle Crystal up again this afternoon and practice over a single jump, see how high you can go. We'll get in as many practice rounds as we can.'

Poppy leapt up, mind racing as she checked all her gear was packed away then untied Crystal to load her onto the truck. She leant in, waiting for Aunt Sophie to put Jupiter on first.

'We're going to win that grand prize, Crystal,' Poppy whispered to her pony, stroking her cheek. Her coat was soft as Poppy ran her fingers down it, before bending to plant a kiss on her dark grey muzzle. 'I know we can do it.'

She was going to help pay off any loan her aunt and uncle had on Crystal by using her savings and winning that money. If the others added their savings too, maybe it could make a difference.

And feed for an entire year! Surely that would go a long way to help. She just had to make sure she won. So what if she was only twelve? It didn't mean she couldn't do it. Aunt Sophie had told her when they'd given her Crystal that she was well known on the competition circuit. Crystal had been a brilliant competitive mount with her last rider, who'd only sold her because she'd turned seventeen and was moving on to a bigger horse. Poppy wasn't as experienced, but her pony was, and it was time to trust in Crystal and let her prove herself.

'Aunt Sophie,' she said in a low voice. 'How much did you have to pay for Crystal?'

'That's not something I want you to worry about, Pops,' Aunt Sophie said, placing a hand on her shoulder. 'But just so you know, we only have another $1500 to pay back on her. She cost a great deal more, but we structured it to pay off all your ponies as quickly as we could.'

Poppy smiled at her aunt, heart racing. If she won the prize money and used her savings, she would come close to paying off the loan. *If there's a will, there's a way*. Wasn't that what Aunt Sophie had just told them?

CHAPTER FOUR

Jump Training

Crystal was probably tired from the big beach ride, but Poppy wasn't going to spend the day sitting around when it was her only opportunity to train. She had the rest of the day before her mum came to pick her up, then they were having dinner with her aunt and uncle, which meant she had a bit longer than usual. After that . . . she gulped. She usually only came to visit every second weekend, but with the competition on next Sunday she was allowed to come back again early on Saturday, so she'd have all day to practise her jumping.

'Poppy, do you want to go first?' Aunt Sophie called out.

'Yes!' she answered. She was cantering in a circle, getting Crystal into a nice balanced rhythm. Katie and Milly were training with her, but Poppy knew she was the only one who wanted this so badly. She was determined to win this event. She gritted her teeth, never having been so sure of wanting something *ever* in her lifetime.

'We're going to pretend this is the actual class you'll be competing in. I want you to take turns, waiting at the edge of the arena until I call you. On the actual day you'll be waiting outside the arena, of course. If you knock a rail, you're out,' Aunt Sophie told them, standing beside the jump in the centre. 'The competition is over when there is only one rider left.'

Katie and Milly trotted to the entrance and halted to watch. Poppy ran a hand down Crystal's neck. Her pony had her head down perfectly, her canter strong yet steady as she circled towards the jump. It wasn't too big, just an average-sized fence with three rails. Poppy urged her on, legs pressed tightly to her sides as they approached.

'One, two three, four . . .' Poppy murmured as they were four strides out. Crystal popped up, stretching out as Poppy released the reins, before landing perfectly on the other side.

'Good girl!' She gave her a big pat and cantered over to the others.

'Milly, you're next,' Aunt Sophie called.

Milly went straight over the fence, too, then Katie. They each did another clear round when the jump went higher. Then it was Poppy's third turn. The jump looked much bigger now, but she remembered her aunt's advice and didn't look at it as they approached, keeping her eyes trained over the poles as if she was looking ahead to the next jump. Poppy gave Crystal more rein, didn't hold her back. It was big, but she knew to trust her horse and let her figure her own strides out.

The jump came up fast and within seconds they were soaring over it. Poppy listened, hoping not to hear the knock of a pole, and they landed without touching it.

'Yes!' she exclaimed. Crystal seemed to sense her excitement and let rip with a buck, which sent Poppy into peals of laughter. 'Crystal!' she scolded. Luckily Crystal hadn't managed to unseat her even though she'd taken Poppy by surprise.

Milly cantered fast towards the fence when it was her turn, and Poppy cringed when Joe's back hoof clipped the top rail and sent it tumbling. Her friend looked disappointed, but she still gave her pony a big pat. Next up was Katie and she cleared it with ease.

They were neck and neck, both doing well, as Poppy cleared the next one. She held her breath when it was Katie's turn, wondering how high they'd end up going. It wasn't that she was getting nervous of the height, they were only training at home after all, but her stomach was full of butterflies at the thought of how high it could go on the day. Would she actually be able to do it?

'Go, Poppy!' Aunt Sophie called.

She gathered up her reins and cantered in a circle before sending Crystal towards the jump. *They had this. They could do it.* Poppy clamped her legs on, staring at the centre of the jump and then forcing her eyes up and past it. Her stomach lurched as Crystal lifted, tucking her knees up high as they cleared it. They landed hard on the other side, the effort of jumping so high feeling completely different to finishing over smaller fences.

'Did you feel the difference then?' Aunt Sophie asked Poppy as she cantered past. 'How much bigger her jump felt?'

Poppy slowed to a trot, then a walk. 'Yeah, I did. It was. Wow.' She shook her head, her heart beating fast. 'It was awesome.'

Sophie's smile was infectious. 'Keep your head up and let her look after you. Crystal knows what she's doing. It's just whether you're confident enough to let her go for it as the jumps get higher. You're doing great.'

Katie went over the fence then, just touching it and causing the rail to wobble. For a moment it looked like it would stay, then it fell to the ground with a thud.

'You win!' Katie called.

Poppy didn't like to see her friend lose, but it felt good to have gone over the jump that many times and not taken a rail. 'Can I go one more time?' she asked.

Aunt Sophie moved towards the jump immediately and put it up, and Poppy cantered towards it. She felt invincible. Like she could conquer *anything*.

They cantered towards it and Crystal thrust her head up, pulling hard. Poppy tried to fight her and stay in control, then glanced up just in time and realised that Crystal had been doing it for a reason, that she needed more rein, was trying to guide them safely towards the fence. Poppy looked down, knowing she'd been too confident and not listened to her horse. Crystal took a quick last stride before gathering herself up, trying her hardest to clear the fence, but Poppy had interfered too much and they took the rail down with them. Crystal's back legs crashed into them and Poppy groaned as she looked behind them and saw they'd managed to tumble two rails.

'I'm sorry,' she muttered to Crystal, loosening the reins until they were on the buckle and giving her a big pat. 'I won't do that again.'

'Trust your pony, Poppy,' Aunt Sophie called. 'She was trying her hardest to get you over that fence.'

Poppy nodded, upset and embarrassed that she'd completely mucked up the last jump. She might have won against her friends today, but she was going to have to do a lot better on the day if she wanted to collect that prize money.

'Want to come for a walk to stretch them out?' Katie asked as she neared them.

Poppy was fighting tears. They were burning her eyes and her throat felt all sticky and hot from trying to swallow them down.

'I'm just going to go for a walk on my own,' she managed to choke out.

Katie and Milly looked at her, worried. But she needed a few minutes alone. Her friends loved their ponies as much as she loved Crystal, but Starlight Stables meant so much more to her and she couldn't stop thinking about losing it.

When her dad had been away serving as a soldier, she'd loved coming here. Then when he'd died, it had been the one place in the world where she could just get away from everything and stop being the girl whose dad had died, the girl who was always sad. Then Crystal had come along, and her aunt and uncle had been so amazing to her and helped her mum when she was depressed and not able to look after Poppy and her little brother.

She owed them so much, and if she could just help out when they needed her, she'd feel so much better. If only she could do something to help them save the farm and not just help to pay off her horse.

She took her feet out of the stirrups to stretch her ankles and patted Crystal's neck as they walked. Her poor pony must be so exhausted from the day they'd had.

'I'm sorry I let you down,' she whispered, her tears falling down her cheeks then onto Crystal's silky grey neck. 'I'm sorry.'

'Poppy!'

She halted Crystal when she heard Aunt Sophie calling her. Poppy quickly wiped at her face, not wanting her aunt to see that she'd been crying. For a girl who never usually cried, she was doing way too much of it this weekend.

'Hey, are you okay?' Concern was etched all over Sophie's face. Her aunt took hold of the reins, standing beside her and looking up.

'I let you and Crystal down,' Poppy said, pleased that her voice wasn't all wobbly with more tears. 'I'm sorry.'

'Sweetheart, you did great. You've never attempted a jump as high as those last two!'

Poppy sighed and absently stroked the top of

Crystal's mane by her wither. 'But I want it so bad. I want to win.'

'Then win,' Aunt Sophie said like it was the most simple thing in the world. 'Believe in yourself and make it happen.'

Poppy sat up straighter in the saddle. 'You really think I have a chance?'

'Yes,' Sophie said without hesitation. 'I do.'

Poppy laughed, her tears long gone now. 'And you're not just saying that because you're my aunt and you have to?'

'Pops, I would never tell you something just because I thought it was what you wanted to hear, especially not when it comes to riding.' She placed a hand on her leg, looking up at her. 'I saw you go over those jumps, and both you and Crystal have what it takes. If you believe in the two of you as a team, truly believe, then anything is possible. Just trust her every step of the way and keep practising.'

Aunt Sophie gave her an affectionate squeeze on the thigh and took a few steps backward.

'Thanks,' Poppy mumbled, feeling a warm glow at the confidence her aunt had in her.

'I'll ride her this week for you, just to keep her

exercised. She'll be rearing to go when you get back here.' Sophie chuckled. 'She'll feel tiny for me compared to Jupiter, but it's always fun having a play around on the ponies.'

Poppy watched her go and then dismounted. She leant into Crystal and gave her a big hug. 'This is our big chance, Crystal. I'm not going to let you down, I promise.'

Poppy led her back to the stables to take off her gear and turn her out in the paddock where the ponies were kept during the week when they weren't being ridden. She wanted to talk to her friends about her plan, but she didn't want to worry them more than they were. They were already upset about what was going on, and there was nothing she could do to help them raise money. But if she could just do her bit to help . . . she wished it were that easy. What she needed to do was text her mum before she came to pick her up and ask her to check her bank balance.

'I don't want to go back to school!' Milly moaned loudly from behind her.

Poppy turned around and made a face. 'Imagine if we could just live here and ride every day?'

Milly grinned. 'If only.'

'We better go pack,' Katie called out from Cody's stable. 'Mils, my mum will be here in half an hour to take us home.'

Poppy sucked in a deep breath. She hoped they would be able to come up with a plan to save their ponies, too.

'See you next weekend,' she said, waving as Milly and Katie led their ponies out to the paddock. 'I'm going to stay here with Crystal a little longer.'

'See ya,' Milly called, blowing her a kiss. 'Can't wait till next weekend!'

'Bye,' Katie waved.

Poppy watched them go, then looked around at the stables. Her aunt and uncle just couldn't lose this place. No way.

'Mum, stop,' Poppy said, running out to the car. She'd been waiting, watching, desperate to speak to her mum before she went inside.

'Hey, Poppy.'

Poppy grinned down at her little brother, his dark curls so badly in need of a cut. He was smiling, like he always was, dimples shining back at her. 'Hey, Tom.'

He sprinted past her, squealing when Casper came bounding out. He loved the dog as much as she did, and within minutes he was rolling around on the grass with Casper in a big bear hug.

'Hi, Mum, great to see you,' her mum said with a laugh.

Poppy smiled. 'Sorry. It *is* good to see you.' She threw her arms around her mother and gave her a quick hug. 'Did you check my bank account for me like I asked?'

Her mum put an arm around her as they headed for the front door. 'I did. But are you going to tell me why you need to know?'

Poppy stopped walking and looked up at her mum. 'I don't want to say anything, in case they don't want you to know, but I overheard . . .'

'Oh, I know what you're going to say. Sophie told me what happened, and she'd already mentioned that they were having some difficulties financially.'

'Mum! How could you know that and not have told me! How long have you known?' Poppy was furious and she bunched her fists at her side, digging her short nails into her palms. How could her mum have kept something like that from her?

'Poppy, I didn't want you worrying about it. It's not something children should have to be concerned about.'

She glared at her mum. 'I'm twelve, Mum. I'm not just a child.' Poppy held her head high, not about to back down. When her mum had been struggling she'd stepped up and done everything – looking after her brother, cooking and making lunches, stopping anyone from noticing that something wasn't right. She wasn't just a kid. 'You should have told me.'

Her mother frowned. 'And what good would that have done?'

'I could have started doing more work! Saving more money!' She took a big breath, not wanting to argue with her mum. 'I can't lose Crystal, Mum. I can't. And I need to pay for her myself.'

The frown on her mum's face turned to a sad smile, and then suddenly she was wrapping her arms around her and holding her so tight Poppy couldn't breathe.

'I'm sorry. I never thought about Crystal, what this could mean for you. I know how much you love her.' Her mum took her hand and held it. 'You have almost six hundred dollars in the bank, which includes the money you got for Christmas and your last birthday. And . . .'

Poppy was happy. It was *way* more than she'd realised, but then she had been doing the dog walking for a really long time, plus helping with other jobs when Old John, the neighbour, had needed help, like when he was planting his new vegetable garden. 'And *what*, Mum?' she asked.

Her mother cleared her throat, and Poppy knew she was just delaying, trying to decide whether to tell her something or not.

'What?!' she asked.

'Your dad had some money tucked away, money that we'd been putting in a jar since we were married. We were always dreaming of going on a special holiday one day, just the two of us.'

Poppy's body went hot then cold. She didn't want to ask, didn't even want to react. She had no idea what her mum was about to say, but . . .

'If it means helping you save Crystal, I'll give

you five hundred dollars. It's a huge amount of money, and I need to keep the rest to cover any emergency car repair bills or to fix things around the house now that your dad has gone. But Sophie and Mark have done so much for us, and your dad would have wanted you to have some of it.'

Poppy couldn't believe it. Another five hundred? 'Ohmygod, thank you!' she squealed, grabbing her mum and jumping up and down. 'Thank you, thank you, thank you!'

That would do it! If she won the competition, plus her own money and the money from her mum, she could actually do it!

'What's going on out here?' Uncle Mark called from the front door. He was standing in his socks, watching them with a smile on his face.

Poppy shot her mum a fierce look and shook her head. She didn't want anyone else to know what she was planning – she wanted to come up with as much money as she could, but she wanted to keep it quiet until she managed to actually do it. It had to help if at least one pony was paid for, and then it would mean Cyrstal wouldn't *have* to be sold.

'I was just telling Mum about how awesome

Crystal's been jumping,' Poppy said. 'I'm so excited about next weekend.'

Mark waved to Tom as he rushed past them into the house with Casper bounding after him. Then he turned back to Poppy. 'Sophie told me how well you've been doing. Said I should place my bet on you in the single jump contest.'

He dodged sideways like he was going to grab her, and Poppy laughed. Uncle Mark was always joking around, but this weekend he'd been so quiet and serious, and seeing him like this made her realise how much she'd missed it.

'Are you going to be there watching?' she asked him.

'Wouldn't miss it for the world. Now how about you go down and show Tom the two koalas in the wildlife hospital while I get your mum a drink and finish off my famous spaghetti and meatballs.'

Poppy groaned. 'Not *your* cooking again!'

'Poppy!' her mum scolded.

She rolled her eyes. 'Seriously, Mum, even though it's yum, there's only so many times you can eat spaghetti.' She grinned at Mark. 'Sorry, but it's true.'

Her uncle only had one dish he could make, so when he was cooking it was the *only* thing on the menu. Poppy laughed and went to get her brother. She was happy to go down to the garage that was doubling as a makeshift wildlife hospital. When her best friend Sarah had been to visit, it had been bushfire season and they'd had a narrow escape from a fire at Starlight Stables. They'd saved a koala named Belinda, who was almost recovered from her burns, as well as another koala that her uncle had taken in. Once they were gone it would go back to being a garage, so she had to make the most of spending time with the gorgeous animals.

'Come on, Tom, I've got something to show you,' she called, already heading back out the door.

Her little brother was a pain in the butt sometimes, but she couldn't wait to see the look on his face when he got to hold and feed an actual koala.

CHAPTER FIVE

Disaster

It had been the longest week ever at school, but finally she was almost back at Starlight. Poppy jumped out of the car the minute Aunt Sophie stopped, seeing Milly already walking towards the stables. Poppy usually caught the train and Aunt Sophie collected her, but today Sophie had picked Poppy up from home because she'd been doing some jobs in Melbourne. Milly and Katie lived a bit closer, so Milly's mum usually dropped them off early Saturday morning.

'I can't believe it's tomorrow!' Milly shouted, running towards Poppy with a big bag over her shoulder.

Poppy couldn't believe it either. 'School was so boring this week,' she moaned, giving Milly a hug. 'Every day just dragged on, but now it's the weekend I'm freaking out big time.'

Milly dumped her bag on the ground outside the stable. 'Come on, let's go get them. I've just had my braces tightened and they're killing me! If riding doesn't make me forget about them I'm seriously going to die.'

Poppy frowned. 'Poor you.' She had no idea how much braces hurt, but it sounded bad.

Milly made a face. 'I only have a few more months to go, but it still sucks.'

Poppy hurried to get Crystal's halter and lead rope, matching her friend's fast walk. They were just heading outside into the sunshine when Milly stopped suddenly beside her.

'Look.'

Poppy stopped and stared, already seeing what Milly was looking at. Sophie was standing in the dressage arena with Prince trotting around her, his beautiful black neck arched gracefully as he seemed to float across the ground.

'Who's that?' Milly asked, pointing.

Poppy snapped out of her trance when she realised that there was someone she didn't know watching Sophie and Prince intently.

'I don't know,' she muttered, knowing deep down that it wasn't good. 'Aunt Sophie doesn't usually push Prince that hard.'

Her aunt had first introduced them to her new young horse, Prince, when Sarah had been visiting Starlight. Prince was going to be Aunt Sophie's new horse once Jupiter was too old to keep competing at such a high level, but he'd only just turned two and Aunt Sophie was very particular about giving him time to grow and mature before doing too much work with him.

'You don't think . . .' Milly started, wide-eyed as her words trailed off and she met Poppy's gaze.

That the other person is a buyer! Poppy knew that was what her friend had been going to say, because it was exactly what she'd been thinking herself. Poppy swallowed hard, feeling like there was a rock in her throat.

Poppy jumped when a hand landed on her shoulder. She spun around.

'Katie! You scared me.'

'Sorry.' Katie moved to stand next to her. 'I thought you heard me coming. I called out. What are you looking at?'

Poppy pointed. 'Prince.'

'Wow, he looks amazing.' Katie sighed in appreciation. Then she frowned. 'I thought Mrs D wasn't working with him yet?'

'She wasn't,' Poppy said with a grimace. 'I hate that everything's changing.'

It was what she'd been worrying about all week, what had been keeping her awake at night and making her wake up with a feeling like she was suffocating, like something heavy was sitting on her chest and stopping her from breathing. She lived for Starlight Stables, for her friends and riding and Crystal. And there was this weird feeling like everything she loved so much was about to disappear, and even though she might be able to pay for Crystal, she couldn't do anything else to help. It hadn't been that long since her dad had died, and Poppy felt like she was about to lose something she loved all over again.

'Do you really think she'd sell him?' Katie asked. 'If it meant saving Starlight Stables and Jupiter?'

Poppy asked. 'I don't think she'd want to, but she'd probably have to.'

'I think so too,' Milly agreed. 'Besides, he must be worth a fortune. Maybe selling him would save Starlight?'

Poppy looked at Prince one last time, watched his elegant trot turn into a big, powerful canter. 'Come on, let's go get our ponies. We need to practise.'

'Can't we just go for a trail ride?' Milly moaned.

'Nope,' Poppy said. 'I'm going to win that money tomorrow, and if I don't, then I want one of you to win it. So that means we're going to jump and jump and jump today to get them ready.'

She took a deep breath, deciding to tell them. 'If I win, I'm going to give Sophie and Mark the money. I reckon we were wrong – any money we put towards our ponies would definitely help.'

She immediately felt better for telling them. They would understand.

'Okay, well one of us has to win then. Good plan. Besides, I wracked my brain all weekend and couldn't come up with anything,' Katie said. 'Let's go get training!'

Milly groaned and Poppy nudged her hard in the side.

'Ow!' Milly howled.

'Toughen up,' Poppy giggled. 'We're going to do this!'

Milly ran ahead a few steps before turning around to walk backwards, looking at them. 'I dare you to jump it bareback. Bet I'll win that one.'

Poppy shrugged. 'I'll let you win that one, just not the single jump contest tomorrow.'

She wasn't usually so competitive, especially with her friends, but she'd never, ever been this determined in her life.

'You really want to do this, don't you, Pops?' Katie asked in a low voice. 'You're desperate to win it.'

Poppy nodded fiercely. 'I would do anything to save Crystal and help Aunt Sophie and Uncle Mark. I just don't see how else I can get the money otherwise.'

'Do you think it will be enough to pay for Crystal?' Katie asked. 'I've been wondering all week how much we'd need to give them, how bad it all is with them.'

'I don't know, but it's got to help,' Poppy answered honestly. She didn't tell them about the other money she had, or that she knew how much was owing on Crystal. Because what if it was a whole lot more on their ponies? It wasn't because she didn't want them to know, just that she didn't want them to worry about the fact that she was able to offer Sophie and Mark some extra money towards Crystal when neither of them probably could.

Katie suddenly burst into tears and Poppy turned to her, astounded.

'Hey, what's wrong?' She put her arms around her. Katie sobbed and Poppy held her tighter. She hadn't ever seen Katie cry before!

'I don't have any money,' she cried. 'I asked my mum and dad but there's nothing they can do to help me. They don't have any extra money. I just love Cody so much!'

Poppy didn't know what to say. And then Milly grabbed hold of them both and was squeezing her as well.

'We're not going to lose them,' Milly said, in her usual bossy voice. 'There's no way Mrs D would let that happen, I just know it.'

Poppy wished she believed that, but she knew that adults often made things sound better than they were. What if Aunt Sophie didn't have a choice?

'Come on, last one to the paddock has to do all the mucking out tonight,' Milly said with a grin.

Katie was still crying but she was wiping away her tears. Poppy pulled a tissue from her pocket and passed it to her.

'Anyone else want to ride them in and race bareback?' Poppy asked.

Milly had already started running. 'Me!' she yelled back.

Poppy reached out and grabbed Katie's hand and they ran together. Once they were riding everything would feel better.

'Go!' Milly screamed.

Poppy wrapped her legs tight around Crystal as they lurched from a halt straight into a canter. They were going fast, too fast for slippery bareback riding, but it was fun and Poppy didn't care if she fell off.

Milly, of course, had raced off just before

shouting *Go*, which meant she was in the lead. But only just.

Joe flew over the jump ahead, his little knees tucked up tight, and Poppy urged Crystal on. They took off just after Joe landed, and Cody was right beside them. She caught Katie's eye as they both cleared it, laughing at the grin on Katie's face.

'No!' Crystal let rip with a buck that almost sent Poppy flying. The only thing saving her was the tight grip she had on her mane and lead rope. Crystal had been a bit too frisky lately!

'Ha ha, beat you guys!' Milly called.

Poppy kept her legs clamped to Crystal, not caring that she'd nearly tumbled to the ground. 'Wanna bet?' She raced past Milly, which sent Joe into a tailspin. The little chestnut reared and bolted after them as Poppy kept watch over her shoulder, but she quickly straightened and kept her eyes on where she was going. They cantered down the paddock and towards the gate, slowing only when they had to. Poppy tried to reach to get the latch, but Crystal was dancing and jumping all over the place, excited from the race.

'Whoa, easy girl,' Poppy soothed, running a

hand down her neck, the other fisted in her mane in case she spooked or bucked again.

'You're a cheat, Poppy!' Milly declared as she rode up beside them.

Poppy grinned at her. 'Me? You're the one who got a headstart the first time around.'

'I want a re-match,' Milly demanded, staying mounted as Poppy slipped off Crystal.

'Fine. Once we're through the gate, we race fair and square.' The look on Milly's face made her groan. 'Oh no. What do you have planned?'

Poppy opened the gate, pushing it wide so she could lead Crystal through, and then held it for the others.

'The show-jumping course,' Milly said. 'We race around it bareback one by one. Whoever doesn't fall off and knocks over the least poles wins.'

Katie let out a big sigh just as Poppy was closing the gate behind them. 'I thought we were supposed to be training properly today?' she asked.

'This would be training. Just bareback instead of saddled up,' Milly said, like she'd thought the whole thing through. 'Then we can prove who the better rider is.'

Poppy glared at Milly. 'Fine. Let's do this.'

'You guys sure this is a good idea?' Katie asked with a groan.

Milly was staring back at them both defiantly, which only made Poppy more determined to beat her. Poppy didn't know what had gotten into her lately, but she'd become so much more serious about winning, about proving herself. Even before her aunt and uncle had told her about their problems, she'd started to think more about winning than just riding.

Poppy vaulted up onto Crystal's back, getting comfortable and securing her grip. Times like this she wished Crystal was a bit fatter or wider – she wasn't that comfy to ride bareback!

'So, are we racing to the start?' Poppy asked.

Milly's stare told Poppy that her friend was as determined to win as she was. 'Paper, scissors, rock for first turn,' Milly said.

Poppy shrugged. 'Sure.' She nudged Crystal with her heels to make her walk up a few steps, so they were facing Katie and Milly. 'Go. Three, two, one!' Poppy threw her hand out flat, at the same time as the other two.

'Ugh, typical,' said Katie.

'Go again,' Milly said. 'Three, two, one!'

Poppy did paper again, and Milly and Katie both did rock.

'Woo hoo!' Poppy cried. She liked the idea of going first, especially while she was all fired up. She knew they could win this!

'Three, two, one,' Milly chanted again.

Poppy watched as Milly beat Katie with scissors to her paper. 'Yes!' Milly squealed.

Ready?' Poppy asked.

'Yep,' Milly and Katie both answered.

Poppy asked Crystal to walk on, then trot, followed quickly by the canter command. It was way too hard to trot bareback, especially when cantering was so much easier to stay balanced to.

They reached the arena in no time, crossing past the stables and down into the larger of the two arenas where all the show jumps were still set up from last weekend's lesson with Aunt Sophie. They weren't as big though, which made Poppy think that some other riding school pupils had been training over them during the week. She'd do anything to be able to ride during the week, even though she knew she should just be grateful she got to come every other weekend.

'Go, Pops!' Katie cheered as Poppy entered the ring.

Poppy kept focused, wanting to pretend like this was an actual competition, that it counted for something. She kept Crystal cantering, her eyes focused between Crystal's pricked ears. They neared the first jump and Crystal took off way too fast. Poppy was virtually powerless to control her speed with no bridle or saddle on, and she started to pull hard on the lead rope that she had tied to Crystal's halter to make pretend reins.

Stop it. Let her go. Poppy was fighting her own thoughts, but as the jump loomed ahead of them she forced herself to let go of the lead rope. *Trust your pony. Let her do it on her own.*

Yes! They soared over, Crystal stretching out as Poppy pretended she had a saddle on. It felt slippery and weird, but she kept her heels planted down, legs staying as close to where the girth should be as possible as she bent forward then straightened as they landed.

'Good girl!' she said, looking to the next jump.

Poppy's heart was beating fast as they approached the second jump. They were going a lot faster than usual or maybe it just felt that way because they were bareback and she was struggling to keep her seat. They popped straight over and headed for the next. There were only seven jumps set up and she was feeling amazing, like they could conquer anything!

They cleared the third, then the fourth, not taking any rails, but Crystal sped up again and took off early for the fifth one. Poppy's stomach lurched as she was jolted forward too fast, landing hard on Crystal's neck. They made it over but she slipped sideways when Crystal shied to the left. *No!* Poppy managed to steady her, to point her in the right direction, but she still didn't have her balance, was trying to correct herself as the jump came at them fast.

'Crystal!' she screamed as her pony cantered faster, their stride all wrong as Poppy clung on as best she could.

Oh no. Poppy knew something bad was about to happen, shut her eyes tight, waiting for Crystal's take-off.

But Crystal never crashed. Poppy was the only one to take off, flying through the air straight over Crystal's head as her pony changed her mind about going over the fence and slammed on the brakes at the last moment.

Poppy tried to curl into a ball to soften the impact. *Boom. Thump. Ouch.*

'Poppy!'

Poppy heard her name being called, tried to lift her head, but she couldn't. *Double ouch.* Every part of her hurt: her head, her back, her arm from where she'd landed.

'Poppy!'

This time she realised it was Milly.

'Stop it,' she muttered, keeping her eyes shut as she swatted at what she thought was Milly. Only this something was nuzzling her and blowing on her face, and Poppy's hand connected with something soft. She peeled one eyelid open and stared into a grey nostril. It was Crystal.

'Is this you trying to tell me you're sorry?' Poppy muttered.

Crystal's face suddenly disappeared and was replaced with Milly's. 'Oh no! Are you okay? I'm so sorry! This was all my fault.'

'Give her space to breathe.' Poppy smiled when she heard Katie's calm voice. She forced her eyes open a crack again and felt better this time.

'Pops?' Milly asked.

'I'm fine, just a bit sore and . . .' She sat up and had to grab hold of Milly's arm. 'Dizzy.'

'You might have concussion,' Katie said matter-of-factly.

'I'm fine. Honestly,' Poppy mumbled, reaching for the side of the jump and hauling herself up. 'Whatever you do, don't tell . . .'

'Girls!'

Poppy let out a loud groan when she heard Aunt Sophie's voice and saw her rushing across the grass, leaping the side of the arena to get to her.

'What's happened? I saw Joe walking off with his lead rope dangling and –' Aunt Sophie gasped, hand to her mouth. 'Poppy! Are you okay?'

Poppy managed a weak smile. 'Fine. I just got winded.'

Her aunt stared at her for a second, then hurried to her side and put an arm around her. 'Tell me what happened. How did you fall? What hurts?'

'Nothing, I mean, I just . . .' Poppy stammered, not sure *what* exactly to tell her.

'Poppy fell off when she was riding the course bareback,' Katie said, not making eye contact with Poppy even though Poppy was glaring at her. Why was she telling Sophie everything! 'She went over Crystal's head when Crystal stopped at a jump.'

Aunt Sophie pulled Poppy closer to her, her body warm. Poppy had been trying to keep her chin up and pretend like everything was okay, but when Aunt Sophie dropped a kiss to the top of her head the tears started, trickling down her cheeks and leaving her gulping for air, trying desperately to swallow them.

'Sweetheart, you need to tell me what hurts. This could be serious.'

Poppy looked up at her, wished she found it easy to lie so she could just tell her that everything was fine.

'Does you head hurt? Is your vision blurry at all? Any dizziness?' Aunt Sophie asked.

Poppy sucked in a big, shuddery breath and furiously wiped away her tears with the back of her knuckles. She was supposed to be convincing Aunt

Sophie that she was fine and here she was crying!

'When I stood up I felt a little dizzy,' she admitted slowly. 'I kind of hurt all over, and I have a sore head. Like it's thumping.'

She watched as Aunt Sophie pursed her lips, her face a mix of concern and anger. 'Would you have told me that if I hadn't asked?'

Poppy glanced at her friends, saw they looked super worried. 'No,' she admitted.

'Because you don't want to miss out on riding tomorrow?'

How on earth could her aunt suddenly read her mind?! Poppy shrugged. 'Uh huh.'

'If you have concussion, Poppy, you can't ride, not without seeing a doctor,' Aunt Sophie said softly. 'I'm sorry, but your health is more important than any competition.'

Poppy felt like she couldn't breathe. Was Aunt Sophie saying what she thought she was?

'I don't . . .' the words stuttered in her mouth. She couldn't even form an answer. *Not ride?*

'Mrs D, this was my fault, not Poppy's!' Milly burst out. 'I'm the one who should be punished! I wanted to beat her and I made her . . .'

'Stop,' Aunt Sophie said. 'This is no one's fault and I'm not trying to punish Poppy.' She sighed, hugging Poppy close again. Poppy wanted so badly to be angry with her, but she just couldn't. 'You girls were having fun on your ponies, and that's great. It's what being here is all about, and none of you did *anything* wrong. But a fall is a fall, and I have to take it seriously.'

'But Mrs D . . .'

'No, Milly, that's my final word,' Aunt Sophie said. 'I'll call the doctor. No one wants to see you ride tomorrow more than me, Poppy. If I can make that happen, I will. I promise.'

Tears pricked Poppy's eyes again, but she refused to give in to them. The show jumping tomorrow meant everything to her. Why had she been so stupid and even jumped bareback in the first place? She was supposed to be practising before the big day, then washing Crystal and plaiting her up to make her look beautiful.

'I'm sorry, Poppy,' Milly said, her voice glum.

Poppy braved a smile, wishing the pain in her head would stop. 'It's okay. It seemed like a good idea at the time.'

'Girls, can you take Crystal back for Poppy?' Aunt Sophie asked. 'I'm going to get her up to the house, give her some Panadol and call the doctor. As soon as she has the all-clear, I'll let her come back down.'

Poppy didn't look back at Crystal or her friends, just let Aunt Sophie guide her back towards the house. It had been the best day ever. And now it was the worst.

'It's going to be okay, Poppy,' Aunt Sophie said.

She leant into her aunt, tucked her head to her shoulder. Sophie was wrong. She just knew it.

CHAPTER SIX

Best Friends Ever

'You need to be honest with me, Poppy. Promise?'

Poppy nodded as her Uncle Mark stared into her eyes. They were seated directly across from one another, Mark with his chair pulled up close to hers.

'I promise.'

She was feeling a lot better after taking some Panadol, which had been gross to swallow down but worth it, and snuggling up in bed under her duvet for a while. But now Mark was home and he had her down in the kitchen.

'You know, I usually can't ask my patients questions, so I should be fine examining you,' he said with a chuckle.

'Mark, I really think we should have taken her in,' Aunt Sophie muttered from where she was leaning against the table.

'I've spoken at length with the doctor,' Mark said. 'Just let me do my thing.'

'If she had four legs I wouldn't be trying to tell you what to do,' Sophie said, sounding exasperated. 'But this is a case for a doctor, not a veterinarian!'

Poppy giggled and bit down on her lip when Uncle Mark raised an eyebrow at her and rolled his eyes. He wasn't taking her fall so seriously, or maybe he just didn't want to upset her.

'I feel fine,' she told him. 'It hurt on my arm when I fell on it, and I bumped my head.'

'Lucky you had your helmet on,' Mark said, reaching for her arm when she held it out and gently touching it, running his hands over every part of it. 'Any of this hurt?'

She shook her head. 'No. It only hurt straight after.' Poppy was telling the truth, it didn't hurt anymore. If it had, she wouldn't have been able to lie to him.

He smiled when he let go of her hand, staring into her eyes now. 'Do you have any pain in your head or eyes? Any blurry vision or anything weird?'

She shook her head. 'Nope.'

He used a small light to shine in her eyes, then ran his hands over her head like he was feeling for something. She was certain there were no big bumps or bruises.

'Poppy, I honestly think you'll be fine to ride tomorrow, but only if you promise to tell us if anything changes. If you get another headache or anything unusual like dizziness, you need to tell one of us.'

Poppy felt like she'd been holding her breath the entire time. When her lungs finally worked again she sucked in so much air it sounded like a big gasp. She tucked a strand of hair behind her ear as she looked from her uncle to her aunt.

'Are you tricking me?' she asked. All this time, right from the moment she'd fallen, she'd expected them to stop her from riding no matter what.

'I'm not tricking Pops, I wouldn't do that to you,' Uncle Mark said, placing a hand on her shoulder.

'Sophie?' Poppy asked, staring at her aunt now.

'I want to keep a very close eye on you, but yes,' she answered, sounding less sure than Mark.

Poppy bit her lip, staying quiet when what she really wanted to do was squeal and leap up and down!

'You need to be careful though, Poppy,' Uncle Mark cautioned.

'I'm really sorry,' Poppy said, wishing she hadn't been so stupid and gone bareback jumping when she should have been more focused on her training. 'I promise I'll be careful and I'll tell you if I don't feel well.'

'Poppy, you didn't do anything wrong. Horse riding can be a dangerous sport, but you were wearing your helmet and you weren't doing anything stupid. It's just one of those things. We want you to have fun here!'

Poppy nodded. Aunt Sophie was right, but she was still annoyed with herself.

'Can I go outside now?' Poppy asked, crossing her fingers behind her back for luck.

Aunt Sophie and Uncle Mark exchanged glances. 'I think you should stay inside for a bit longer. Rest a bit more, then head out after the girls have had their lesson.'

Poppy wanted to argue that she was fine, but

she didn't dare in case they changed their minds about her competing the next day. 'What if I just came down to watch the lesson? So I don't miss out on what you're teaching?' she said in her sweetest voice.

Aunt Sophie laughed. 'Fine. You can come down, but no riding until tomorrow!'

Poppy giggled. 'Hand on my heart.'

'Go on up to bed for another half hour. It'll do you good to get some rest.'

Poppy jumped up and raced for the stairs.

'Slow down!' Uncle Mark yelled after her. 'I said to take it easy, didn't I?'

Poppy wasn't used to going slow, but she did as he said. There was no way she was doing *anything* else that might ruin her chances of having a shot at winning the prize money tomorrow.

'What did they say?' Milly hissed as Poppy ran up behind her and fell into step beside her friend. Milly was leading Joe, and Katie was just ahead of her.

'Katie!' Poppy whispered as loud as she could.

Katie spun around and clamped her hand

over her mouth, eyes wide. 'You scared me! I was daydreaming.'

'What are you doing down here?' Milly asked.

Aunt Sophie was already in the arena. Poppy had spotted her earlier when she'd been trying to figure out where everyone was.

'I'm not allowed to ride today, but I can compete tomorrow,' Poppy told them. 'All I can do is watch your lesson.'

'Ugh,' Milly groaned. 'I remember what that was like. It sucked when Joe was injured and I had to sit and watch without riding.'

'Girls, mount up please and warm up those ponies.'

Poppy gritted her teeth, wishing she had Crystal saddled up. Her poor pony would be thinking she'd been abandoned. 'Have fun.'

Katie threw her a sad smile and Milly frowned before mounting Joe. She watched her friends ride into the arena, walk around for a while, then start to trot. After a while she glanced at her aunt and noticed that she was waving at her. She squinted into the sun and put her hand up to shield her face. Was she waving her over?

'Poppy!' Aunt Sophie called.

Duh, she was definitely waving her over. Poppy went to run but stopped herself, walking fast so that her aunt didn't tell her off. She always sprinted everywhere, wasn't used to going slow, but she needed to be on her best behaviour this afternoon.

'Do you need me to do something?' Poppy asked when she finally reached her. Walking took ages!

'Yes, as a matter of fact I do.'

Her aunt was giving her a weird kind of grin and Poppy planted her hands on her hips. Something was up, but in a good way.

'I thought you might like to take the lesson since you can't ride.'

Poppy burst out laughing then bit down on her lip. What? She stared at her aunt. 'Are you serious? You want me to *take* the lesson?'

Aunt Sophie's smile was wide as Poppy stood there gaping at her, realising that her aunt wasn't kidding.

'Of course I'm serious. If you can't ride, you can at least think through the jumps and instruct Milly and Katie. You know the theory, and I believe in you.'

Poppy wrapped her arms so tight around her aunt that she tried to wriggle out of Poppy's grip.

'This is crazy. I can't believe it,' said Poppy.

'Don't make me change my mind,' Aunt Sophie said with a laugh. 'Besides, I might need you to start taking some lessons for me when you turn thirteen.'

Poppy squealed and jumped up and down.

'Girls, Poppy will be taking the lesson today and I'll be observing,' Aunt Sophie called out. 'Finish warming up and then listen out.'

Poppy's cheeks were hurting she was smiling so hard. 'Thanks. This is awesome.'

'By the way, your friends have been pretty busy while you've been up at the house. You might want to look in on Crystal as soon as we finish up here.'

Poppy had no idea what Aunt Sophie was talking about, but she was super curious. She started to think about Crystal, about what they could have done. She wished she was riding her right now.

'Poppy?'

She blinked and saw that Aunt Sophie was watching her expectantly. 'Oh, sorry!'

Poppy turned all her attention to her friends, hoping they didn't mind being the guinea pigs for her first lesson as an instructor. She'd helped out heaps with the summer camp kids, but they were little children. These were her friends and they were easily as good as her at riding. Which meant she had to focus and not let them down when they so needed this training session to count.

'Okay,' Poppy called out, making sure her voice carried loud enough. She hated having a lesson when she couldn't hear her instructor clearly. 'The course has already been set out, and I'm going to time each round. Time is going to count tomorrow, so I want you to focus on making the turns tight and getting to each jump as quick as you can.' Neither Kate nor Milly gave her a weird look or questioned what she said, and it helped to boost her confidence. 'Milly, you're up first. Aunt Sophie, can you time for me?'

'Sure thing, Pops,' Aunt Sophie replied.

Katie fell back and rode towards Poppy, but Poppy quickly switched her gaze to Milly. Joe was super fast, but sometimes he was too quick for his own good.

'Keep him in check just enough, to make sure that he doesn't take off too fast. Sit up tall, shoulders back!' Milly soared over the first jump and Poppy grinned. 'Great work!'

She watched as they sped around the rest of the course, glancing quickly over at her aunt. Poppy hoped she was doing okay. She didn't want to be too bossy, but she also wanted to say what she thought rather than stay quiet.

'Great work!' Poppy called as Milly neared the final jump. 'Keep your eyes up!'

The top rail on the final jump wobbled when Joe just knocked it, but it stayed put.

'Woo hoo!' Milly cheered.

'You're up, Katie,' Poppy said. 'Try to push him a bit faster, legs on and turn those corners as tight as you can.'

Katie gave her a salute and cantered off, clucking Cody on. Poppy focused on her, saw the way she pulled Cody up a little to slow him down as they approached the first fence. She couldn't believe how much like her aunt she sounded when she was giving instructions!

'Trust him, Katie. Don't hold him back. Ride him forward, legs on.'

Poppy smiled when she saw Katie follow her

advice, propelling him into a faster canter. This time when they approached she didn't slow him down and Cody jumped it easily, going straight back into his canter when he landed.

'Great work! Keep your legs on!' Poppy cheered.

Poppy was brimming with pride when Katie finished her round clear, having easily jumped every fence. She knew without checking her watch that Katie had done a fantastic time, too.

'Who won?' Poppy called over to her aunt, who was standing at the edge of the arena. Both Katie and Milly had ridden clear, so it only came down to time.

Her aunt walked closer, a big smile on her face. 'Katie by two seconds.'

'Yippee!' Katie had just halted beside Poppy and her squeal made Poppy jump.

Milly laughed from behind Poppy and Poppy grinned at Katie. 'Congrats. You rode really well.'

'And you taught really well!' Katie insisted. 'I mean, *really* well. I forgot it was you.'

'Yeah, I hate losing but you were good,' Milly admitted. 'Can we go again?'

Poppy was about to say 'yes' when Aunt Sophie

placed her hands over her shoulders and spoke up.

'I actually think that's enough, girls,' she said. 'Both of your ponies did everything you asked, so you can end on a good note without pushing them too hard. It's a big day tomorrow.'

Katie glanced at Poppy and giggled. 'Are you going in to see Crystal now?'

Poppy frowned. 'What's going on?'

Katie shrugged, and when Poppy glanced at Milly, she also shrugged.

'What is it?!' Poppy asked.

'You'll have to go and see.'

Poppy glanced at her friends again and then her aunt, before turning and bursting into a fast sprint. She ran as fast as she could back towards the stables.

'Poppy, no running! Slow down!' Aunt Sophie yelled after her.

But Poppy didn't care. She was feeling fine and she was going to die if she didn't see what they were talking about *right* now. She skidded on some hay in the entrance, letting her eyes adjust to the dimmer light inside. The concrete floor was littered with a bit of hay so she did slow down, not wanting to slip or scare the horses. Crystal's stall was past some of the bigger horses, and when Jupiter hung his head over the wooden half door to say hello, she didn't even stop, just put her hand out to him as she kept walking.

'Crys-*tal*!' she called out in the sing-song voice she always used when she said her horse's name. 'Come on, girl.'

Poppy's boots stopped at Crystal's stall. Her jaw dropped as she stared at her pony. Crystal had poked her head out and was nickering, her brown eyes on Poppy.

'No way,' Poppy whispered. Crystal always looked pretty, but right now she looked amazing. Her grey neck was arched and her entire mane had been braided into perfect plaits then wound into perfect rosettes. Even her forelock had been done.

Poppy walked slowly towards her, holding out her hand, not sure whether to laugh or cry. She couldn't believe her friends had done this for her!

'Wow,' she whispered. She let herself in, her eyes locked on her horse's mane. Katie and Milly had known how much she wanted her plaited, to have her looking perfect, and they'd done it for her while she'd been stuck up at the house.

Crystal looked incredible.

Poppy ran a hand down her gleaming coat, moving around her body. And then her eyes fell on Crystal's tail. She gasped. It was plaited too! That had to be Aunt Sophie, because only her aunt knew how to do the intricate reverse braid.

Tears sprang into Poppy's eyes and she threw her arms around Crystal's neck.

'We're going to do it,' Poppy mumbled, her lips against Crystal's soft hair. She inhaled the sweet smell of her pony. 'You look like a champion, and I promise not to do anything to muck it up.'

It was time to trust her horse. Poppy had never, ever been so determined in her life. And it helped that she had the best friends ever in the whole world.

CHAPTER SEVEN

Ready, Steady, Go!

Poppy wasn't used to feeling so nervous, but today she was a bundle of nerves. Her tummy was churning and her palms were so sweaty that she kept having to wipe them on her jods.

'Come on, girls, let's go watch the demonstration class,' Aunt Sophie said as she walked out of the horse truck.

Poppy glared at the name on the side of the truck, hating the feed company that had let her aunt down. If they'd just kept sponsoring her, Poppy wouldn't be freaking out about having to win the money she needed.

She looked away. Right now she had to just

focus on her showjumping round.

'Just a sec,' she called, going back to double-check Crystal's lead rope. The knot was secure and Crystal was happily munching on some hay, tied up with Joe on one side and Cody on the other. They hadn't brought any other horses or riders with them today, although some of Aunt Sophie's pupils were competing with their own ponies.

'Can you believe how big some of those jumps look?' Milly asked, her eyes wide when she looked back at Poppy. 'It's insane!'

They had a way to walk over to the arena, but even from where they were standing it was obvious how big the jumps were. Aunt Sophie was waiting for them up ahead, chatting to someone Poppy didn't recognise, and they all ran to catch up with her.

'I thought you'd like to watch the demonstration and then we can walk the course,' Aunt Sophie said. 'I've heard this part is going to be very cool.'

'Please give a warm welcome to our brightest local talent in show jumping, Caitlyn Winters!' the announcer said, the sound crackling and squeaking from the megaphone.

A stunning bay horse entered the arena at a canter, his black tail held high, dark-brown coat gleaming. The rider held her hand in the air as she rode past, circling the entire arena. Her horse's neck was curved, beautifully on the bit as he moved gracefully, and Caitlyn hardly looked like she was moving an inch in the saddle, her body so at one with her horse. Then they approached the first jump and everything changed.

The elegant horse raised his head and sped up, his legs moving fast as he raced. The jumps were massive, the biggest Poppy had ever seen up close, but the horse and rider made it look easy. Caitlyn was incredible, letting her horse go fast but keeping him in check enough before each jump so that they didn't rush it. The compact gelding cleared each fence with ease and the rider's position was perfect as she bent forward and released the reins every time they jumped. The final fences loomed, a double, and they bounced straight through.

The crowd gathered around the arena started to clap and Poppy quickly glanced sideways as she joined in. Her friends looked as in awe as she felt.

'And that's why she's this year's Young Rider

Champion and member of the Young Rider Elite Squad! Let's hear it for Melbourne's own Caitlyn Winters!'

The crowd clapped and whistled again as she exited the arena, and Poppy stared after her. Caitlyn was on the Young Rider Elite Squad, which meant she was probably still a teenager. Maybe twenty years old at the most. It was Poppy's dream to make that squad one day, and seeing Caitlyn Winters in the flesh had only made her more excited.

'Why is there a car being driven into the middle of the arena?' Poppy heard Katie ask.

'You'll have to wait and see,' Aunt Sophie replied.

'Poppy, look!' Milly squealed.

Poppy looked back to the arena and saw two of the jumps being moved at the same time as a rider entered the ring. She gasped. The driver was leaving the car, and Caitlyn had entered again, her horse nowhere near as calm as he'd been earlier. She cantered slowly but her horse was hyped up now, which meant she battled to keep him steady and he kept throwing his head up high in the air.

'I can't believe she's going to jump a car,' Poppy

mumbled, shaking her head in disbelief. She was *actually* going to do it.

'She's crazy!' Katie hissed.

'No, she's freaking awesome!' Milly said.

Poppy watched as Caitlyn cantered in a circle and popped over a smaller jump before approaching the car. It was a Holden and it wasn't small, the bright red paintwork glinting in the sun. Poppy held her breath, terrified till the last second, before watching the bay soar over the car and land with a thud on the other side before cantering off like they'd done nothing out of the ordinary.

'Woo hoo!' Milly cheered loudly beside her.

Poppy clapped as hard as she could. If Caitlyn Winters had been awesome before, now she was the most amazing rider in the world.

'If you weren't convinced about this fantastic team before, there is no doubting them now. Join me in wishing them good luck at the Australian Jumping Champs!'

Poppy was still clapping as they left the arena, and long after. She only stopped when she realised that everyone else had. She could hear the other two talking to her aunt, but she was still in a state of total awestruck wonder.

'Let's go take a look at the course,' Aunt Sophie said.

Poppy pulled herself out of her thoughts and forced her feet to cooperate. She could dream about what she'd seen all night – right now she had a job to do and she had to focus. Winning meant everything to her today, and nothing was going to stand in her way.

She followed after the others, pausing only when an immaculate palomino pony cantered past and almost rode straight into her. Poppy gulped at the shiny horse, his rider as perfect as he was.

'Don't even think it,' said her aunt, flashing her a grin.

'I don't know what you're talking about.' Poppy smiled back.

'You're thinking that rider is better than you because her pony is flashier and her gear is all perfect. But that's not true.'

Poppy gulped and refused to look back at the pretty palomino again. Aunt Sophie was right, you couldn't tell anything from looks alone, but still . . . today wasn't going to be easy. No way.

'They're just finishing the course now, adjusting the height for your class,' Aunt Sophie said, back in instructor mode. 'I want you to walk up to each jump, ask me any questions you need to, and pace out the space between the double and the triple.'

Poppy nodded and walked straight up to the first jump. It was fairly simple, an upright that shouldn't cause Crystal any worries. She wasn't so worried about this course, because she should be able to get around okay – it was the next class that had her all nervy.

'We're going to blitz this,' Milly said confidently.

Poppy rolled her eyes. Milly was always crazy confident.

'I don't know about blitz it, but it's nothing we haven't trained for.'

'You girls will be fine. It's probably going to come down to speed because some of the other riders will have been showjumping for some time.'

Poppy knew what she meant – some of the riders would have been on the same pony for years, practising and competing regularly, whereas they hadn't been at this level for long.

'Today is going to be fab, I just know it,' Katie

said, a smug-looking smile on her face.

'You say that like you know something we don't,' Poppy said.

'I just believe in us, and I have a really good feeling about the jump-off.'

Poppy felt her eyebrows shoot up, surprised that Katie was so unusually confident.

'Let's walk it as a team first, then you can go back through again on your own if you want,' Aunt Sophie said.

Poppy focused and ran a little to fall into step beside her aunt. She needed to listen to every piece of advice Aunt Sophie had if she had any chance of doing well today, let alone winning. The jumps also seemed bigger when she was on foot instead of in the saddle, but she wasn't going to worry.

'Do you remember how to pace out each jump?' Aunt Sophie said.

Poppy stuck her hand up. 'Yep. Our ponies are about three big human strides to one of their strides.'

Aunt Sophie gave her a thumbs up. 'That's right. I do three normal strides, but you girls would need to do three big strides for a pony your size.'

Milly ran on ahead, approaching the double. 'Can I pace out this one?'

She didn't wait for anyone to answer, just ran around to the rear of the first jump and stepped it out.

'That's three strides!' Milly called out.

'I know you can trust Milly because she's your friend, but it's a good habit to always stride it out yourself rather than relying on anyone else. That way you get your own feel for the jump and pacing, plus sometimes not everyone is trustworthy if they're a fellow competitor.'

'Yeah, imagine if we'd ever trusted *Jessica*,' Poppy said with a laugh.

The other two groaned, which was what Poppy always did just at the mention of the mean girl's name.

'Did you get three strides too, Poppy?'

Poppy finished the last of the nine big steps that equalled three pony strides. 'Yep.'

'Good. Now let's quickly walk the rest of the course so you can recall the order.'

It was Poppy's biggest fear, forgetting her way or getting confused about which jump to go over when she was riding. As soon as they finished the course, she walked it quickly again on her own, and then stood back and ran through the jumps in her mind, eyes darting to each one as she mapped out her course. There was nothing to be nervous about. *Yet.*

Poppy checked Crystal's girth for what felt like the hundredth time. She had her sweaty palms back and she was getting all jittery again.

I can do this, I can do this, she chanted over and over, trying to pep-talk herself and failing. If she hadn't fallen the day before, if she hadn't missed out on her lesson with Aunt Sophie after a week away from riding, if . . . *ugh, enough with the ifs!*

Poppy threw the reins over Crystal's head and mounted, feeling better when her bottom landed in the saddle with a familiar gentle thump. She pushed her feet through the stirrups, checked the length was right, then gathered up her reins.

'Come on, girl, let's go,' she told her horse. As she rode past the truck she gave Katie a quick smile when their eyes met. They were both focused on what they were doing and hadn't spoken much while they'd prepared the horses after walking the course. Milly had already gone off to warm up.

'Good luck out there,' Katie called out.

'You too,' Poppy replied.

Within minutes Poppy had joined the other riders and horses warming up in the big grassy paddock adjacent to the horse-truck parking area. There were so many horses circling around – walking, trotting and cantering – that she felt overwhelmed. Poppy reached down and stroked Crystal's neck, wanting to touch her pony to settle herself, to remind her of why she was doing this.

'We need to win. We need to ace this,' Poppy whispered to Crystal.

She took a deep breath that filled her lungs, then slowly let it go as she nudged Crystal on with her heels. Her pony wasn't wanting to walk and started to jig-jog, all excited about the commotion going on around them. Just as she asked Crystal to trot on, a horse sped past them, missing them by inches, the whoosh of the other horse's body forcing Poppy to pull up Crystal hard.

'Hey!' she yelled out. It was too late, the rider

was long gone, but the way she'd zoomed past her like that wasn't okay.

'Poppy!'

Turning in her saddle, Poppy glared at another horse that cut its way too fine past her. Then she locked eyes on Milly riding towards her.

'Just remember what Mrs D said about warming up,' Milly shouted.

Poppy wracked her brain and couldn't remember anything!

'What?' she shouted back.

'Block everyone else out, find your own space no matter what, and get on with the job!'

Milly's grin was infectious and Poppy gave her a quick thumbs up as her friend turned to ride away. Milly was first up out of the three of them, which was why she'd been first to start warming up.

Block everyone else out.

Poppy kept repeating the words over and over in her head, even as riders glared at her for riding through their circle or getting in their way. It was impossible not to with so many riders competing for space, but Poppy shrugged it off. She started to trot, smiling when it all came back to her. When she'd been grumpy about being sidelined after her fall and watching Katie and Milly have their lesson the day before, Aunt Sophie had told them only to worry about themselves, and that was exactly what Poppy was going to do.

She pushed Crystal into a trot. 'No,' she murmured when her pony tried to break into a canter. Poppy kept the trot at the speed she wanted by not letting Crystal make the decision for her, rising up and down slowly until she got what she wanted. Eventually Crystal put her head down and accepted the bit, but it felt like she was about to explode beneath her! Poppy only had to touch her leg to her horse's side for her to burst into a canter, so she concentrated on keeping her calm and ignoring the interruptions of other riders and horses misbehaving.

'Whoa!'

A big chestnut reared almost right beside her when he veered out of control. Poppy slipped her outside leg back and kept her inside on the girth to ask for a canter again and Crystal obliged, giving a half-hearted buck this time.

'Hey, be good,' Poppy scolded, trying not to

laugh. She had no idea what was up with Crystal and the bucking, but she was pretty sure it was only when she was super-excited, which was a lot lately.

She put Crystal through her paces, cantering first on the left rein and then on the right, before attempting to go over the practice jumps. There were only two jumps set up near the middle of the paddock, and Poppy was relieved to see that one of them wasn't too big. The adult classes were well underway and the bigger horses were easily clearing the larger of the two fences, and she crossed her fingers that there weren't any ponies from her class training over that one.

Block everyone else out, she told herself. She squared her shoulders and cantered towards the jump when she saw her chance. Crystal fought to go faster and Poppy let her, knowing that when the time came they were going to have to go quick to win. Their canter was fast but it wasn't out of control, and they soared over the fence.

'Watch it!'

Poppy pulled Crystal up when an older rider snapped at her. She ignored her, not about to let someone shake her confidence. She hadn't done anything wrong and it was the same track everyone jumping the practice fences had to take.

'Good girl,' Poppy praised Crystal as they rocketed into a canter again, falling in behind another horse. They popped straight over again a second time when it was their turn, not quite as fast this time, and Poppy decided not to practice any more. Crystal was warmed up and jumping well, and she didn't want to drill her too hard.

As she let go the reins to let Crystal stretch out, Poppy spotted her aunt. She was waving out with her hand above her head, trying to get her attention, so Poppy trotted over to her, still riding on a loose rein.

Aunt Sophie was dressed in her usual crisp shirt, this time a soft pink one, but paired with tight jeans tucked into her boots rather than jods since she was just watching and not riding for once.

'You looked great out there,' Aunt Sophie praised her when they halted beside her.

Poppy grinned. 'Thanks.'

'I'm proud of the way you found your own space and did your thing. Sometimes that's the scariest part of competing when you're out and about.'

'This is the final rider in this class, then it's you guys,' Aunt Sophie told her. 'You ready?'

Poppy nodded even though she wasn't convinced she'd ever be ready. Her stomach was doing the crazy butterflies trapped and beating their wings thing again, but she tried to ignore it so Crystal didn't feel how nervous she was.

'Hey!' Milly announced loudly.

Poppy held her whip out and grinned when Milly tapped hers against it.

'Nice riding out there, Milly,' Sophie said. 'I'm not going to call Katie over because she's up last. I'll let her stay focused for a bit longer.'

Poppy took her feet out of her stirrups and let them dangle, trying to relax. Then she tipped forward in the saddle and slung her arms around Crystal's neck to give her a big hug. Her soft mane always calmed her, and she stroked her and kept her cheek pressed to her neck, breathing slowly. She would have been nervous anyway, even if the stakes weren't so high.

Aunt Sophie's hand suddenly touched her shoulder. 'You're going to do great.'

Poppy gulped. 'You really think so?'

Her aunt squeezed her shoulder. 'I know so. You've got a great pony and I trained you myself, so you have to be brilliant.'

Poppy returned the big smile her aunt flashed her, before sitting up to watch the first rider in her class. All up, there were thirty or so entries, and the first pony was a pretty buckskin. They did a nice round but they looked slow and knocked a couple of rails, and before she knew it another rider was entering the ring, this time a solid little bay. It refused the first jump and ended up disqualified after three refusals at the double.

'Maybe we do have a decent chance,' Milly muttered from beside her.

Poppy had her gaze firmly fixed on the entrance to the ring, and she watched as a polished-looking black pony with white socks entered at a canter. 'Don't speak too soon,' Poppy murmured back.

'Oh crap,' Milly whispered.

Poppy bit her lip hard as she watched the perfect pony and equally perfect rider soar over every fence. The black gelding had his legs tucked up high, knees popping up tight as they jumped every fence clear. The rider let out a whoop after clearing the last fence and dropped her reins to hug her pony.

'Ugh, I can't even hate her,' Milly muttered. Poppy laughed. Her thoughts exactly. The rider had been pitch perfect and she'd given her pony a whole lot of love, which meant there was nothing not to like.

'Man, I'm jealous.'

Poppy turned to look over her shoulder and saw Katie and Cody right behind them. They had obviously walked over during the round and Poppy had been concentrating so hard she hadn't even realised they were behind her.

Crystal shifted her weight to her other back leg, happy resting and watching. 'Yeah, I'm jealous too. She was amazing.'

Milly let out some sort of *hmph* sound and Poppy laughed. She bet Milly was super jealous too.

'Sweetheart, you're up next,' Aunt Sophie said to Milly. 'Want me to walk over with you?'

Milly shook her head confidently. 'I'll be fine, thanks Mrs D.' She rode off at a trot as Poppy stared after her.

'Bet she'll do great,' Poppy said. Milly was an awesome rider. She always did well and got over the jumps, if a little too quick sometimes. She was all about speed, whereas Katie was all about jumping faultlessly, which meant she sometimes didn't get recognised for how amazing she was because of her time. But now that they'd been training more and Katie had been letting Cody go faster, Poppy was guessing that she was going to be tough competition. Both of them were.

'Go, Milly!' Katie yelled when Milly's number was called over the speaker system.

Aunt Sophie was clapping and Poppy dropped her reins to do the same. She realised she was holding her breath, and she let it go as Milly entered the ring at a trot, quickly breaking into a canter and circling before going through the flags and heading for the first jump. She was over it without being even close to touching a rail, and as they sped around the rest of the course Joe was perfect, clearing every single jump and going quick, too. Poppy shook her head, trying to shake away the thoughts she was having. She wanted Milly to do well, she never ever wanted her friends to do badly, but just this one day she wanted to be the best.

Poppy cheered as her friend cantered past them.

'Woo hoo, go Milly!' she shouted.

Katie was clapping and calling out too, and Milly held up her hand and waved before slapping Joe in a big pat on the neck and joining them, a huge smile stretching across her face. Milly's cheeks were flushed red, curls escaping from the bun beneath her helmet even though she'd had her hair perfect earlier in the day.

'You did great, Milly. I'm so proud of you,' Aunt Sophie said.

'There's three riders before me now, so I think I'll go have a trot around,' Poppy announced, deciding that she'd be better off riding than just standing around. Besides, she didn't want Crystal to be relaxed instead of all excited about their turn.

'Good luck,' Milly said, still grinning. 'It's so much fun, I wish I could do it all over again!'

'With the round you just did, I bet you'll be in the jump-off,' Aunt Sophie said. 'There's a new rug up for grabs for this division.'

Poppy's eyebrows shot up but she didn't say anything. She wasn't going to be super greedy, just the big cheque and the feed for a year was enough, but a pretty new rug would be nice too!

'Good luck, Pops,' Aunt Sophie said.

'Yeah, good luck,' Katie said.

Poppy rode off without glancing back, head held high.

CHAPTER EIGHT

Jump Time

Poppy trotted back to the practice area. There weren't nearly as many riders training now, so she cantered Crystal in a circle then popped over the jump, before trotting then slowing down to a walk and heading closer to the ring. She rode along the far side, just walking. But Crystal was hyped up and knew what was about to happen, so it didn't take long for them to get there. She was pretty sure there were still two riders ahead of her.

'Name?' a woman shouted, flapping one hand in the air like she was trying to fly, the other hand clasping a clipboard. 'Rider, what is your name?'

Poppy gulped. Was she talking to her?

'Poppy Brown,' she called back in a loud voice.

'We've been waiting for you. Hurry up!' the woman scolded.

'But I thought there were . . .'

'Hurry up!' the woman interrupted. 'We've had a rider scratched from the program so you're up!'

Poppy kicked Crystal in the side harder than she should have, upset that she was late and wishing she'd just walked over instead of going over the practice jump again. Crystal reared and Poppy only just had time to grab a handful of mane and throw her head back to avoid getting a broken nose.

'Crystal!' she told her off, desperately trying to hang on. Crystal landed and pawed the ground and Poppy put her legs on firmly. 'Get on with it,' she muttered.

The woman pointed to the ring and Poppy had to bite her tongue not to snap, 'Yeah, yeah, don't get your knickers in a knot.' She rode in and breathed deeply, refusing to get all rattled because things weren't going to plan.

Crystal shied at something the second they entered, but Poppy had felt how jittery she was and had her heels planted down hard, her reins short enough to give her control.

'It's okay, girl. Whoa,' she said in a calm voice, hoping it soothed her pony. They finally settled into a steady canter and Crystal seemed to relax a little, although she was still fighting to go faster.

Ding-ding.

The bell rang and Crystal leapt into action, throwing her head up in the air and trying to charge off. But Poppy refused to let her take charge. She pulled her in a tighter circle, forced her to slow, before looking towards the first jump and pointing her between the flags. Crystal's canter quickened and before she knew it they were over the first jump.

Poppy forced herself to look ahead, to always look at the next jump, and soon they were over the second fence, then the third. They hadn't knocked a rail yet and Crystal was going fast enough that she was sure their time was good.

Finally they approached the double and Poppy checked Crystal, made her slow down just a little before letting her do her thing.

'Ugh!' she gasped as Crystal stumbled, her front leg tripping on something and throwing them off balance.

Poppy knew it was all wrong, she'd lost her reins and had nothing to hold except the buckle, but Crystal had hardly slowed and suddenly the jump was there. Poppy shut her eyes, ready to fall, certain they were about to crash through the upright, but Crystal started to lift off the ground and Poppy instinctively grabbed a handful of mane, tried to be as graceful as she could so she didn't throw her pony off balance. *No way!* They landed, and Poppy quickly gathered her reins up as much as she could in the quick three strides before they took off again, somehow clearing the second of the two jumps with ease.

'Go, Crystal!' she screamed wildly, praising her horse and patting her as they headed towards the second to last jump, a spread that looked as big from her pony as it had from the ground. They soared over it, and then the last, and then they were cantering through the finish line.

'Woo hoo!' Poppy felt amazing. Her heart was racing, her hands shaking from the crazy almost-crash they'd had. She patted Crystal's neck over and over as they trotted past the lady with the clipboard and around the ring back to where Aunt Sophie and her friends would be waiting for her.

'Amazing!' Aunt Sophie declared the second she stopped beside them. 'Poppy, that save was incredible!'

Poppy's cheeks felt hot and she knew her face was blood red. 'I thought we were going to crash,' she admitted. 'But the save was all Crystal's.'

'That was pretty cool,' said Milly.

Poppy was listening to Milly but it was her aunt she was staring at. The smile on Aunt Sophie's face, the way she was looking back at her, made her feel so confident because she could see how proud her aunt was.

'Poppy, you did exactly what I told you to do,' Aunt Sophie said in a low voice. 'You let your pony save you instead of interfering with her, and she got you safely over the jump. If you hadn't listened to her and trusted her, Crystal would have crashed.'

Poppy nodded. She'd known it was close, that it could have gone either way, but she'd also remembered what she'd been taught, knew how good and clever her horse was.

'No pressure, Katie, but I think I already have two in the lead here!'

They all giggled and Katie flopped dramatically over Cody's neck.

'You'll kick butt out there, don't worry,' Poppy told Katie.

'Ha ha, famous last words,' Katie muttered back. But Poppy could see how excited her friend was and knew she'd be fine. Out of all of them, Katie was always the best prepared and the most practised.

'You know, I really needed something to make me feel good, so thanks, girls,' Aunt Sophie said. Poppy realised she was close to tears. 'You've made me very proud today.'

'What did I miss?'

Poppy spun around in the saddle. 'Uncle Mark! You made it!'

He held his hands up in the air and made them all laugh again, tears forgotten. 'So who's winning? I don't have to pick favourites, do I?'

Trust Mark to make them all feel good. Poppy had almost forgotten about the big jump-off later in the day, but seeing Mark here reminded her of what was to come. He'd promised to be there to watch when Aunt Sophie had told him how determined she was to win.

'Katie, you're up soon,' Aunt Sophie said as Mark moved up beside her and put an arm around her shoulders. 'I think you should head over.'

Katie rode away and Poppy didn't take her eyes off her. They were a striking team, Katie and her pretty palomino, and Poppy knew they'd do great.

Poppy was between Katie and Milly, their ponies lined up side by side as they stared at the centre of the ring. The secretary for the competition was standing beside a man with a megaphone, and they were all waiting to hear who had placed in this round. The top ranked riders would go into a jump-off, which meant that Poppy could be competing three times in the one day. Poppy gulped at the thought. *Ahead of the big jump-off.*

'The ribbon ceremony will be later in the day, but the top six riders will be going into a second round against the clock, sponsored by FrostBreaker Horse Rugs. The winner will receive a new rug of their choice from FrostBreaker's new season collection.'

Poppy dug her nails into her palms. She had

stuffed her gloves into her pockets because her hands had gotten so hot and sweaty. It was only early summer but the day had turned out warm and blustery, the trees around them swaying back and forth. She held her breath when the announcer paused, listening to the crackle of the speaker, waiting to hear if she'd made it.

'First place is Addison Lane!'

A small crowd on the other side of the arena started clapping, and Poppy saw straightaway that it was the beautiful black gelding with the white socks and the immaculate looking rider. Poppy clapped too, disappointed not to have won but appreciating what an amazing round the other rider had had.

'Second place goes to Milly Walker!'

'What?!' Milly's scream frightened Crystal and made her jump, which almost made Poppy fall off because she'd been resting with her feet out of the stirrups and not holding the reins.

'Whoa,' Poppy soothed, grabbing hold of the reins and steadying herself before turning to Milly.

'Congrats, you so deserved that,' Poppy told her, holding her hand up for a high-five.

Milly looked like she was about to jump out of

her own skin she was so excited.

'Great work, Mils,' Katie said.

'There was only a second between second and third place, so we'd next like to congratulate Poppy Brown!'

What? No freaking way!

'Wow,' Poppy managed to stammer as Milly flapped her arms so hard Poppy was sure she was about to take off.

'Poppy, woo hoo!' Katie squealed.

Poppy quickly glanced at her aunt and uncle, and saw their huge smiles as they clapped loudly. She was so proud that she'd done so well, and that Milly had too. At least Sophie would know that her training had worked!

'You're the best, Crystal,' Poppy whispered to her pony, stroking her neck. They might not have won, but they'd done better than Poppy could have even dreamt a few months ago.

They announced fourth and fifth place, and Poppy sat up straighter, forgetting about patting Crystal as she waited. Poppy's whole body was on edge and she held the reins tighter, waiting, listening.

'Katie Richards takes out sixth place!'

'Yes!' Poppy hissed under her breath at the same time as Milly cried out the word.

'It's official, we've all made it,' Poppy said. She couldn't believe it. 'We've actually done it.'

'Not yet,' Milly said. 'I want that pretty rug. And I'm going to get it.'

Poppy exchanged glances with Katie. She'd never seen Milly this serious or determined about anything other than trouble-making before, and it showed Poppy what strong competition she was. Joe was a quick pony, too, which made him perfect for this type of timed trial. But Crystal was consistent and clever and her knees tucked in so high when they jumped, making her a true superstar, so she wasn't going to let it rattle her confidence. Poppy knew she was still in with a shot for the big jump-off. She plastered a smile on her face as her aunt and uncle congratulated them.

'Could the top six riders please prepare to re-enter the ring. Sixth place goes first!'

Poppy gathered up her reins, knowing she would need to give Crystal a light warm-up again. 'Good luck, Katie.'

Katie gave Cody a quick pat. 'I'm kinda nervous.'

'Me too!' Poppy admitted.

Milly didn't seem to be suffering from the same bout of nerves. She was off at a trot and doing her thing. Poppy wished some of it would rub off on her, although maybe it already had. Maybe that was why she was so determined all of a sudden.

As she trotted, then cantered, letting Crystal stretch out and warm up her muscles, Poppy noticed Aunt Sophie talking to a man she hadn't seen before. He was gesturing widely and smiling, and her aunt looked happy, but Mark had his arms folded, his expression way more serious than usual. Poppy felt a now-familiar churning in her tummy, but she forced the feeling down. Surely it wouldn't be bad news, not here, and the man didn't look all mean and cold like the ones from the bank.

'Watch out!'

Poppy turned her attention back to what she was doing just in time to see the rider on the perfect black pony come flying towards her.

'Eeek!' Poppy managed to turn Crystal hard out of the girl's way.

'Sorry! I couldn't stop him!'

Poppy waved out as the other rider cantered in a circle around her. 'No problem.' Maybe the pony wasn't as perfect as he looked. From the way he was throwing around his head and chomping on the bit, she was guessing he turned on the charm in the ring and could be difficult otherwise.

'Good luck!' the girl called.

Poppy smiled back. Milly was right, this rider was impossible to hate even if they were all jealous of her. 'Yeah, you too.'

And then she saw Katie in the ring and she slowed Crystal to a walk and headed back. It was almost show-time again.

'Go!' Poppy whispered to Crystal as they shot through the flags and hoofed it towards the first jump. She had her legs firmly to her pony's side, body upright but tipped forward slightly in jumping position as they flew over. Poppy wasn't going to slow Crystal down and she wasn't going to interfere with her, just point her in the right direction and trust that she'd get them safely over each fence.

She knew they were going faster than Katie had

gone, and Poppy didn't just want to get around, she wanted to win. They soared over the next jump and the next, and Poppy tuned everything out, focused on every jump. She listened to the sound of Crystal's hooves as they landed, gripped the leather reins and kept her eyes up.

'We can do this, come on, girl!' she said to Crystal, not caring who could hear her. 'We're almost there!'

Crystal seemed to sense her excitement and grunted as she took off over the first of the double, easily zipping between the jumps and flying over the next. Then they were over the second to last, then the last, and Poppy thrust her reins forward as they raced the rest of the way to the finish line.

'Yes! We did it!' she whispered, patting her on the neck, her smile hurting her cheeks it was so wide. 'Clear again!'

Milly was up next and they passed each other. Joe was hyper and dancing sideways, but Milly looked like she either had him under control or didn't care.

'Good luck!' Poppy called out.

'Ha! As if I'm gonna beat that!' Milly cried back.

Poppy halted as soon as she left the ring to watch her friend. She gasped as Joe looked like he was going to stop at the first, then did a massive jump to clear it like it was double the size it actually was. Then he zoomed around the rest of them.

'No!' Poppy groaned as Milly took a rail, then another, as they headed too fast into the double. They were so fast, but Joe got a little too excited sometimes, just like his rider.

When Milly finally exited, Poppy flashed her a big smile. It had still been a great round.

'He looked strong out there,' Poppy said as a breathless Milly pulled up beside her.

'He just about yanked my arms off!' Milly moaned.

Poppy laughed and positioned Crystal beside Joe. They stayed mounted to watch the final rider, the one on the pretty black gelding. Poppy fought the urge to cover her eyes, knowing that if they stuffed up at all, Poppy might have a shot at winning. *As if that's gonna happen.*

'What's the bet she'll ace it?' Milly sighed.

Poppy didn't say anything until the round was over and the girl and her gelding went all clear.

'She's amazing.' She was starting to have her doubts that she'd be able to beat this rider in the jump-off, but she was trying hard not to think about it.

Milly had turned already and started to head back to the others, and Poppy did the same, following her at a walk. She was so proud of Crystal, and she knew her aunt would be, too.

'I timed all the rides, girls,' Aunt Sophie said.

Poppy halted. 'And?'

Aunt Sophie's grin was huge. 'I think it's going to be close for first place. I timed the last rider as being a second or two faster than you, but the official time might be different.'

Poppy had to stop her mouth from hanging open. 'Seriously?'

'Yep, seriously,' Aunt Sophie said.

Poppy looked at Katie, then at Milly, dumbstruck.

'That means you'll be second if you don't win,' Katie said, as if Poppy hadn't figured out what her aunt meant.

'She's not dumb!' Milly laughed.

Poppy dismounted and her aunt threw her arms around her. 'You're so close, Poppy. I really, truly believe that you're amazing.' Aunt Sophie looked around at the girls. 'You all are. You've made me so proud.'

Poppy glanced at her watch. Only an hour to go until the big jump-off.

'Come on, Mark's gone to get lunch ready. Who's hungry?'

'Me!' Poppy answered in unison with her friends.

The other two dismounted beside her and they all led their ponies after Aunt Sophie and headed for the truck.

CHAPTER NINE

The Jump Off

Poppy was munching on a hot dog that Mark had bought for them when she remembered the man Aunt Sophie had been talking to earlier. She finished her mouthful.

'Hey, Aunt Sophie, I saw you talking to someone before. Was he a parent?' Poppy didn't want to sound too nosey without having a reason to ask. 'I thought he might have been watching the black gelding.'

Aunt Sophie looked up and smiled. She didn't look worried; in fact, she looked more relaxed than she had in days.

'He's actually the director of FrostBreaker

Horse Rugs. He was here to personally give the winner from your class the rug,' Sophie said. 'He recognised me, that's all.'

Uncle Mark laughed and Poppy spun around to eyeball him.

'What's so funny?' she asked. She looked at Milly and Katie but they were chatting with their heads bent together, so it wasn't like anyone else was in on the joke. 'Why are you laughing?'

'Nothing,' Mark said, but Poppy could tell he was lying. 'It's just that coming here with you girls today was a stroke of good luck.'

Poppy was puzzled. 'I don't understand.'

Aunt Sophie shook her head and glared at Mark, which only made Poppy more curious. She hated secrets!

'Poppy, that man is interested in sponsoring me. He thinks I'm a good fit for the company, and he said that if I place top three at the dressage champs I could consider it a done deal.'

'No way!' Poppy jumped up, so excited. 'That's amazing!'

'What's amazing?' Milly asked.

Poppy saw that they'd stopped talking and were

staring at her like she was loony.

'I'm going to get ready for the jump-off,' she blurted, desperate to make the day even better.

'Poppy, don't get too excited for me,' Aunt Sophie cautioned, her hand closing over Poppy's wrist. 'We haven't discussed the finer details, but it's a step in the right direction. A big step.'

Poppy threw her arms around her aunt and gave her a quick hug. 'He'd be crazy not to sponsor you.'

'Well, I'm glad you think so.'

Aunt Sophie kissed her head and then Poppy ran off to get Crystal ready. It was now or never.

It was time. Poppy had already watched a few other riders, and there weren't as many in this class as her last one. It seemed not everyone was giving it a go, but the lack of numbers wasn't helping Poppy's nerves at all. *Maybe I should just canter off in the other direction ... No, you can do this!*

She shortened her reins and prepared to go. Crystal snorted as she held her back, and when it was their turn they settled into a steady canter and easily cleared the jump. They repeated that three more times, with only one rider being knocked out of the class. The next round they lost three more riders, the jump seeming a lot higher than when they'd first started, and Poppy's heart started to pound when she was one of only ten riders left.

'It's not that big,' she muttered to Crystal as the jump went up another notch. *Who am I kidding – it's huge.*

When it was their turn again she pushed Crystal into a canter, keeping her reins short enough to have contact but without holding her pony back. They cantered fast and Crystal took off perfectly, clearing it with ease. Poppy gave her a quick pat, and just as they halted she heard the crash of a rail and realised the rider after them hadn't gone so well. *It must have been Milly. At least Katie's still in.*

A groan echoed through the crowd when another rider took a rail.

Poppy glanced to her left, then right, saw that they were down to seven after that round. The next rider dropped a rail too. *Six.* Including her.

'Go girls!' Uncle Mark was cheering from the sideline and Poppy gave him a quick wave. He was always so goofy and fun, and the way he was jumping up and down made her forget how nervous she was for a moment.

'And here we go again!' The scratchy voice came through the loudspeaker without any warning and made Crystal startle.

'Whoa, you're okay,' Poppy told her as she settled her mare, one hand to her neck, the other firmly holding the reins. 'It's almost our turn again.'

She grimaced when she looked up just in time to see the first horse refuse, putting on his brakes and almost sending his rider flying over the rail without him. Then it was Katie's turn and Poppy watched as she cleared it. Another rider knocked a rail, the black gelding aced it, and then it was Poppy's turn. She didn't do anything different this time around, just let Crystal work her magic. Her pony tucked her legs up high, the movement of her body flying through the air feeling bigger than usual, just like it had when they'd been training at Starlight over the larger fence. They landed without touching a pole. *Yes!*

The final rider took a rail, which meant there were only three of them left now. She gulped. How had they done this well against such amazing riders?

'Good luck,' the rider of the black pony said out of the blue.

Poppy smiled. 'You too.'

Katie wasn't looking at her, seemed completely focused, and this time around Poppy wasn't so sure they were going to clear the jump. The three horizontal red-and-white striped poles looked like pretty candy canes. But this time they were so high.

It was Katie first, and as she cantered towards it and Cody took off, Poppy was certain she was going to clear it. But Cody's back hoof just clipped it. The rail rolled from side to side before eventually tumbling to the ground.

'And third place goes to Katie Richards!' the announcer said, the screech and crackle of the loudspeaker making Crystal lurch sideways. Poppy wished they'd stop using the stupid thing!

'You did great, Katie,' Poppy called out as her friend left the ring. And then it was time for the black pony, who cleared it so easily he made it look like jumping a Cavaletti.

Poppy swallowed hard, taking her time, not wanting to spook Crystal with her own nerves.

'Here goes nothing,' she whispered as they set

off towards the jump.

Poppy stared at the centre of it, almost hypnotised by the size of it; the bright poles drawing her gaze. But then she remembered her lessons. She quickly raised her eyes and let Crystal speed up. Three strides, two, one . . . lift off!

They flew through the air and Poppy glanced behind her when they landed, amazed that the top rail was still up. She burst out laughing. How was she still in the competition, against one of the best riders she'd ever competed against? It was crazy!

The jump went up again and she gulped. It was scary high now. Luckily the black pony had to go first.

Poppy shoved her fist into her mouth, biting down on it as the pony lifted off the ground, only just clearing the big upright. Then it was her turn. She sucked in a big breath and then they were heading towards the jump. *I can do it. Crystal is amazing. We are going to make it.*

'Eeek!' She couldn't help squeaking as they took off. Crystal had never jumped so big! Poppy thrust her reins forward, releasing them all the way so Crystal could stretch her neck out and get them over. She glanced down, saw that they were clearing it, then they landed and the impact was bigger than she'd ever felt before. Poppy straightened in the saddle, unable to wipe the smile off her face. *We did it!*

Then it dawned on her that the jump was about to go higher. What if they both cleared this one and then it had to go even . . . *Stop thinking. Stop thinking. Just jump.*

Poppy stayed quiet and still as she watched the jump go up again. It was like her body had completely frozen to the saddle.

The black gelding quickened his pace before he approached, stretching up high, looking like he was going to just clear it. Then his hoof clipped the rail. It rattled and Poppy gasped. *Ohmygod. No way.* She shut her eyes tight. There was no thump.

Poppy opened her eyes and saw the rail was still moving. Then it fell slowly to the ground.

It had been so close, but if she jumped clear this last time then the prize was hers!

Poppy looked down at her hands, watching them shake. She held the reins tighter, clasped her gloves around the leather. Crystal reared, only going halfway up, but Poppy knew it was because she could feel her nerves. Crystal's heartbeat was probably matching hers, which was super-fast right now!

'We've got this,' Poppy told Crystal in a voice that sounded way more confident than she felt. There was so much on the line. So much riding on this one jump. If she won, she could pay for Crystal, make sure her pony wasn't sold if things didn't work out for Aunt Sophie and Uncle Mark.

Poppy stared at the jump, clamping her jaw shut tight and deciding that there was no way they were taking a rail. 'Let's go!' she told Crystal at the same time as they started to canter. She made her pony go faster, kept her eyes focused over the jump and refused to think about anything other than clearing it like they were riding for gold at the Olympics.

They sailed through the air. Crystal had her ears flat back instead of pricked, the jump by far the biggest they'd ever attempted. And they'd done it! They'd gone straight over without taking a rail!

'Woo hoo!' screamed Poppy.

'Congratulations goes to Poppy Brown riding Crystal!' This time when the loudspeaker squeaked and crackled, Crystal didn't seem to care. They cantered around the arena and Poppy thrust one fist into the air. She'd won! She'd actually won! She couldn't even listen to what else was being said, everything was a blur as she kept cantering.

When she finally slowed and pulled up beside the rider on the black pony, she couldn't help but grin at her even though she didn't want to make her feel bad for losing.

'Great ride. Congrats,' the other girl said.

'Thanks!' Poppy beamed, finding it impossible to wipe the smile from her face. 'I wanted it so bad. It means I won't lose my horse, that I can pay for her.'

The other girl's smile got even bigger. 'Are you serious? You were actually riding for your life out there?'

Poppy nodded. 'Yeah, I guess I was.'

'Then I'm glad you won. I'm Addison by the way. And that was my sister Scarlett who was knocked out before your friend.'

'Poppy,' she replied. 'Your pony is gorgeous. And you're so lucky that you can ride with your sister.'

They stood together as someone official-looking ran over and then someone else with a massive cheque like the ones Poppy had seen on TV game shows. Aunt Sophie came rushing over then, as well as another woman that Poppy guessed was Addison's mum.

'Poppy!' Aunt Sophie called out. 'I can't believe it!'

Poppy laughed. Neither could she.

'Could our winner please come forward to collect the first place prize of five hundred dollars, as well as a year's worth of feed from HorseNuts!'

Poppy wasn't sure whether she was supposed to be on her pony or dismounted, but she decided to stay on. Suddenly there were people all around her, fussing and talking and she didn't know what to do, but she was pleased she was still in the saddle. A big sash was tied around Crystal's neck and then Aunt Sophie took over, fussing and standing at Crystal's shoulder as someone else took their photo with a man holding the cheque beside them.

She'd done it. It was taking a while to sink in – her heart was still racing like crazy and her whole body felt all hot and weird. The jump-off was over.

She could stop thinking about it, stop worrying about it, stop staying awake at night. It was finally over.

'You're the best horse in the world,' she told Crystal as she dropped forward to sling both arms around her neck.

Things were looking up. She was going to be able to give Aunt Sophie the money to pay Crystal off, and there was a pretty good chance that her aunt was going to have a sponsor soon. But it didn't mean Joe and Cody were safe *yet*, or the farm. She glanced over at her friends, who were shrieking and jumping up and down in excitement.

Tonight they would be going home before Poppy, and no matter how excited she was, she didn't want them to know about her paying for Crystal before Aunt Sophie had a new sponsorship deal. Because what if the farm wasn't saved? What if . . . she gulped, pushed the thoughts away. She'd wait until they were gone, then she would tell Aunt Sophie and Uncle Mark.

Right now, she just wanted to enjoy the big ribbon around her pony's neck.

CHAPTER TEN

Saving Crystal

'You look like you're up to something.'

Poppy sat down at the kitchen table across from her aunt and uncle. The other girls had just gone, and she was absolutely bursting with excitement. She sat on her hands, had them planted under her bottom to try to stop herself from wriggling. Poppy hadn't wanted to do this while Katie and Milly were around, and now it was finally time.

'I need to tell you something,' she said, suddenly as nervous about what she had to say as she'd been before the jump-off!

'Spit it out, Pops,' Uncle Mark said, frowning. He sipped his coffee but his eyes never left hers.

'I . . .' She took a big huff of breath. 'I want to give you the five hundred dollars I won to help pay for Crystal.' Her aunt opened her mouth to say something and Poppy quickly spoke before she could be interrupted. 'I know it's not enough on its own, but I also have other money saved up, plus some money that Mum has given me to help. It makes almost one thousand five hundred dollars all up, and I want to pay the loan off for you.'

Poppy blinked away tears and bit hard on her bottom lip, annoyed that she was about to cry.

Aunt Sophie rose and sat beside her, taking her hand. Her eyes were full of tears too. 'Sweetheart, you don't need to do that.'

Poppy nodded. 'Yes, I do. I love her and I know you've done so much for me and I want to give you the money. So I don't have to ever worry about her being sold.'

Uncle Mark cleared his throat and she looked up. 'Poppy, I don't want to take your money, but you're right. That would completely cover the loan on her.'

'But you need to understand that selling Crystal was never something we were going to do,' said her aunt. 'Not unless we absolutely had to, and I would have fought so hard before I ever let that happen.'

Poppy hugged her aunt. 'I know. But I want to do this. I want to help you because you've always helped me when I needed it.'

Aunt Sophie returned the hug, holding her tight. 'We love you so much, Poppy. There's nothing we wouldn't do for you, and it's *supposed* to be the adults doing the looking after!'

Poppy grinned. 'I'm not just a hopeless kid, you know.'

'Oh, we know that!' Uncle Mark said, grinning.

Aunt Sophie stared at Poppy, long and hard. 'You were so determined to win that competition, Pops. I've never seen you so full of fire, so desperate to win.'

'All I could think about was saving Crystal,' Poppy replied with a shrug. 'I had to win.'

She hadn't been one hundred per cent confident *all* the time, but in the end she hadn't let her nerves get the better of her.

Uncle Mark reached over and took her empty glass of Milo.

'She was always your pony, kid, with no strings

attached. But what you've done means she'll never ever risk being sold.'

Poppy laughed. 'Good.' It was exactly what she'd wanted to hear.

'But you are giving us that year's worth of feed, too, right?'

Aunt Sophie gave Mark a shove. He grabbed her in return and planted a kiss on her cheek with a big smacking sound that made Poppy laugh harder. She knew the farm wasn't safe yet, but Crystal was hers and she planned on keeping her fingers and toes crossed until the big dressage day.

'Do I still get to be your groom at the dressage champs?' Poppy asked, following Aunt Sophie into the kitchen.

'Of course. I'm counting on you.'

'And,' Poppy started, struggling to say the words, 'will you have any other options if this sponsor doesn't come through?' She was feeling so great about Crystal, but if there was no Starlight Stables . . . it wasn't even worth thinking about.

'Don't worry, Pops,' Aunt Sophie said as she loaded the dishwasher. 'It will all work out, just you wait and see.'

Poppy hated waiting. But she didn't really have a choice.

The horses were all incredible. Poppy stood in awe, watching as they trotted and cantered and practised a million dressage moves that made her jaw drop. Chestnuts, bays, greys, palominos . . . they were all gleaming with perfect tails and immaculate plaits and massive movements.

Just staying an extra night at Starlight and travelling in the early hours to the show in the horse truck with her aunt and uncle had been exciting, but this was crazy incredible! Ever since hearing about last year's champs held in Sydney she'd been desperate to see what it was like, and already she was in awe of all the riders.

'Earth to Poppy.'

Poppy spun around. *Oops.* So much for being Aunt Sophie's super-attentive groom.

'How do I look?'

She looked Aunt Sophie up and down. 'Um, *amazing.*'

Her jods were white, her jacket was black with

shiny gold buttons, and her hair was tucked up in a hairnet, only the back bit showing beneath her hat.

'Have you seen him yet?' Poppy asked. She'd been frantically trying to spot the man from the showjumping day but everyone was starting to look the same to her.

'No,' Aunt Sophie said firmly. 'And I don't want to. I need to focus on my first test and not think about anything else.'

Poppy got it. This wasn't just about the sponsorship for her aunt. It was about doing well enough to retain her ranking, to give her a serious shot at being selected in the next Olympic team.

'Can you finish getting Jupiter ready for me, please?'

Aunt Sophie disappeared and Poppy took off Jupiter's halter, which she'd had secured over his bridle. She took hold of the reins and reached up to stroke the big chestnut's silky coat, running her hand down it over and over again. He was so beautiful, easily as stunning as any of the other big Warmbloods going through their paces in the warm-up area.

'You can do this,' Poppy whispered, leaning in

and pressing her cheek against him. 'You're the best horse here, okay? Don't you forget that.'

'What are you whispering over there?'

Poppy gave Jupiter a final hug before checking his girth and putting the reins over his neck for her aunt, thankful that he'd ducked his head to make it easier for her. 'I'm just telling him how amazing he is. Just to make sure he knows what's expected today.' The night before, when she'd been helping to prepare Jupiter while Aunt Sophie sewed in his plaits, Poppy had whispered the same thing to him.

'Ha ha, believe me, he knows!' Aunt Sophie said with a laugh. 'I've talked to him non-stop ever since this all happened.' Poppy watched as her aunt approached Jupiter, her touch always light and her manner with him so kind. 'The poor horse probably just wants some peace and quiet instead of the ear bashing he's been receiving.'

Poppy passed Aunt Sophie her whip after she'd mounted, smiling up at her. 'Good luck, Aunt Sophie.'

'Thanks, Pops.'

She stayed standing beside the truck, her eyes never leaving Jupiter's muscled rump as he walked off to join the other horses. Poppy knew the drill – they'd warm up for about twenty minutes, then there would be the first test, and then the freestyle to music. That was the one that always made Poppy excited, seeing the beautiful big horses 'dancing' to the music as they trotted and pirouetted and cantered around the arena. She'd watched as her aunt had run through the test the morning before.

'Hey!'

Poppy spun around to find Milly and Katie behind her, their faces flushed from wherever they'd run from.

'Want to go find a good spot to watch from?' Milly asked. 'There are, like, so many people here.'

'No, you go on without me,' Poppy said. 'I need to stay near Aunt Sophie until she rides in, just in case she needs something.'

She had to remember that she was Sophie's go-to girl for whatever she needed, since she was actually her groom for the day. Even though she'd already picked up horse poo, filled the haynet for when Jupiter returned, and done all the errands Aunt Sophie had needed her to do before she started riding, Poppy still needed to stay near. If anything happened, she was the one Aunt Sophie would call on.

'Okay, see you soon,' Katie said. 'I don't want to miss a second.'

Poppy walked off on her own so she'd be near where her aunt was training, glancing back at the truck and imagining new signage across it. Aunt Sophie was going to win, she had to, and then everything would be okay.

CHAPTER ELEVEN

Jupiter the Great

'Do you think she'll win?' Katie asked, sounding breathless as they whispered and watched the last part of Aunt Sophie's test.

Poppy sucked in her bottom lip and chewed on it. As soon as her aunt had entered the ring, she'd sprinted off to sit with her friends. 'I don't know. So long as she makes top three she'll be happy, I reckon.'

Jupiter's canter was magical, the way he moved jaw-dropping as he did a series of flying changes across the diagonal of the arena. Then he was cantering down the centre line and finishing with a perfect halt.

Aunt Sophie took off her hat and saluted, which sent the crowd into mad applause. She was local for Melbourne and she was obviously one of the crowd favourites.

'Far out,' Poppy muttered. *That was amazing*. She'd seen Sophie ride so many times, but seeing her actually compete had been incredible.

She jumped up and left her friends, running towards the arena. A big bay trotting towards her made her stop, and then she fast-walked so she didn't spook any of the horses. Sophie was just dismounting by Mark when she reached them.

'That was amazing,' Poppy told her.

'Thanks,' Aunt Sophie said. 'That was definitely the ride of my lifetime. Jupe was such a good boy!'

Poppy took the reins from her aunt's hand. 'Do you want me to walk him?'

'Please,' Aunt Sophie said. But Poppy noticed she wasn't looking at her while she was talking, that her aunt's gaze was going straight past her. Then she reached for Mark.

'He's there and he's coming our way.'

'I'll start walking, cool him down,' Poppy told them, knowing exactly who they were talking about.

She didn't want to be in the way. 'You did great out there. Best ever.'

Her aunt's smile was huge. 'Thanks. I thought so too.'

Poppy had tied Jupiter up and rugged him up, as well as offering him water and giving him a small feed. He looked content standing there, and she flopped down inside the truck with Katie and Milly. Being groom was fun, but it had also been a lot of hard work. All they could do now was wait.

'I don't ever want this to end,' Katie said, her voice sounding dejected.

'Me neither,' Milly grumbled.

Poppy didn't say anything. She just wanted to know. She knew that Sophie and Mark would fight hard to keep the farm and the riding school, not to mention all the horses, but still, it wasn't going to be easy. She'd heard them talking enough to understand that.

'Girls!'

Poppy jumped up. It was Uncle Mark calling them. 'In here,' she called back. She poked her head out the door and beckoned for her friends to join her.

'We have good news,' Mark said, beaming at them.

Poppy quickly exchanged glances with the other two. 'Did we miss the announcements?'

'No, but we've reached a deal with FrostBreaker. They're going to sponsor Sophie based on the ride they've seen today. They love her.'

'Where is she?' Poppy asked, not wanting to get too excited yet, even though her heart was hammering away like crazy.

'Chatting to the rest of the FrostBreaker team who came to watch her, sipping champagne and waiting for the winners to be called,' Mark said. 'They want to come and meet Jupiter afterwards, so Poppy you might have to get him gleaming again. Sorry, kid.'

'I don't mind!' Poppy would happily groom him all day if it meant keeping the farm.

'Sophie and I have made the difficult decision to sell a half share in Prince, which means we won't be able to retain full control over him or his future, but it's a small price to pay. As soon as this deal is signed on the dotted line, we'll be okay. I promise. In fact, we'll be in a better position than we were before.'

Poppy squealed and grabbed her friends' hands. 'Really?'

'Really,' Mark said firmly. 'I wish you girls had never found out in the first place, it wasn't fair to worry you, but everything's going to stay the same. Your ponies will always have a home at Starlight Stables, and I hope you'll be staying with us for years to come. Okay?' Mark frowned. 'But no boyfriends, just horses, you hear me?'

Poppy nodded and laughed when Milly giggled.

'Come on, let's go find Sophie. She was desperate for you three to know the good news.'

Poppy dropped her friends' hands and threw her arms around Mark. 'Thank you,' she whispered.

'For what?' Mark asked.

'Just everything. I don't know what I'd do without you and Sophie.'

'And Crystal,' he said with a chuckle. 'I know we come second to her.'

He was right, she loved Crystal more than anything in the world, but Uncle Mark and Aunt Sophie were pretty awesome, too.

'Let's go!' Milly cried.

Poppy raced off after her, trying not to run. She laughed, knowing how stupid she must look doing her fast walk, but she didn't care. Starlight Stables was safe. Crystal was safe. All the other horses still had a home. That was all that mattered.

ABOUT THE AUTHOR

As a horse-crazy girl, Soraya dreamed of owning her own pony and riding every day. For years, pony books like *The Saddle Club* had to suffice, until the day she finally convinced her parents to buy her a horse. There were plenty of adventures on horseback throughout her childhood, and lots of stories scribbled in notebooks, which eventually became inspiration for Soraya's very own pony series. Soraya now lives with her husband and children on a small farm in her native New Zealand, surrounded by four-legged friends and still vividly recalling what it felt like to be 12 years old and head over heels in love with horses.

HORSE TERMS

A female horse is called a filly until it is four years old and then it's called a mare. A male horse is a colt until four years old before being called a stallion. Unless a stallion is going to be used for breeding purposes, most young male horses are castrated by a veterinarian and are then called geldings. Geldings are better behaved than stallions and easier to control!

AUNT SOPHIE'S SUPER WARMBLOOD DRESSAGE HORSE, JUPITER, IS A HUGE 17.2 HH.

Warm-blooded horses are popular in high-level dressage competitions for their big movement and athletic builds, with the most commonly known Warmbloods being Dutch, Belgian and Swedish Warmbloods, Holsteiners and Trakehners. They are most suitable for confident, experienced riders.

THE FIRST BOOK IN AN EXCITING AND ENJOYABLE
AUSTRALIAN SERIES ABOUT THE FRIENDSHIP AND
ADVENTURES OF THREE HORSE-CRAZY GIRLS.

PONY DETECTIVES

Poppy is thrilled to be back doing the one
thing she loves – riding horses at Starlight Stables –
especially when her aunt and uncle make all her
dreams come true with a gift of her very own horse.
But there's a catch . . . Poppy must look after the new
scholarship girls. Will the bold and troublesome
Milly and shy, sensible Katie be the pony-mad
friends she's always hoped for? When horses go
missing from the local farms, Poppy worries about
Crystal, her new horse. Will the girls be able to
protect their ponies from the horse thief and find
the missing horses at the same time?

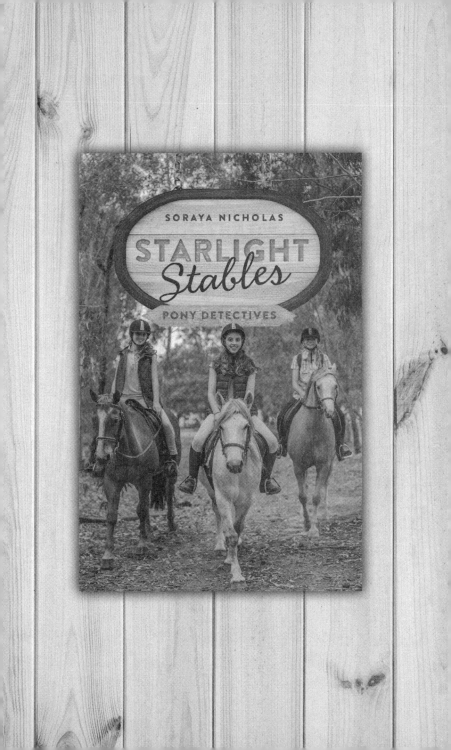

GYMKHANA HIJINKS

Horse-mad friends Poppy, Milly and Katie
are overjoyed to be back at Starlight Stables and
spending every second with their new ponies –
riding, training and having fun while preparing
for their first big Pony Club competition. But when
a rival competitor arrives one day to train with them,
trouble seems to seek the girls out at every turn.
Is it just coincidence? Or is someone trying to
sabotage the three friends' chances of winning?
Can Poppy, Milly and Katie expose their
rival's risky antics in time to save their
chances at the gymkhana?

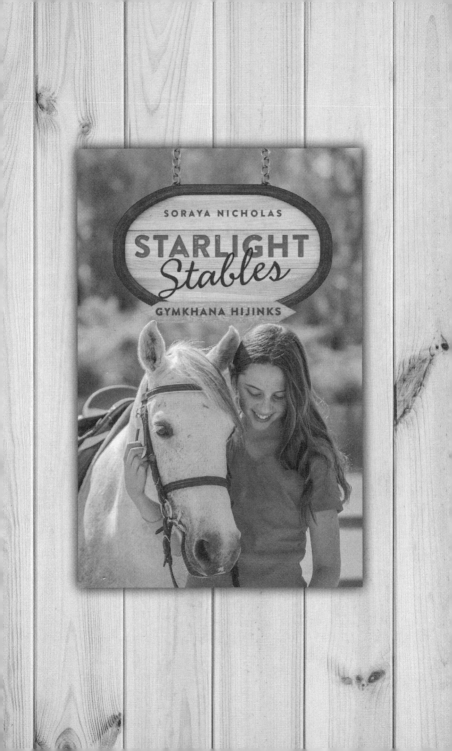

BUSH BOLTS

Poppy is so excited. Her best friend
Sarah is finally coming to visit Starlight Stables.
She is sure that Sarah will love it all as much as
she does – especially Poppy's beautiful pony,
Crystal, and her horse-mad friends, fiery Milly
and sweet Katie. But it soon becomes clear that
Sarah doesn't share Poppy's love of horses and
riding – in fact, she's more interested in helping
Poppy's uncle with some injured animals.
When a bushfire erupts nearby, Poppy finds
herself fighting not only to save her friendship but
also to save her beloved Starlight Stables.
Will she lose everything she loves?

SORAYA NICHOLAS

STARLIGHT
Stables

BUSH BOLTS

ACKNOWLEDGEMENTS

Penguin Random House would like to give special thanks to Isabella Carter, Emily Mitchell and India James Timms – the faces of Poppy, Milly and Katie on the book covers.

Special thanks must also go to Trish, Caroline, Ben and the team at Valley Park Riding School, Templestowe, Victoria, for their tremendous help in hosting the photoshoot for the covers at Valley Park, and, of course, to the four-legged stars: Alfie and Joe from Valley Park Riding School, and Carinda Park Vegas and his owner Annette Vellios.

Thank you, too, to Caitlin Maloney from Ragamuffin Pet Photography for taking the perfect shots that are the covers.

FOR MORE INFORMATION ABOUT THE

STARLIGHT STABLES

Series

DON'T FORGET TO VISIT

www.sorayanicholas.com